The Bride of Sforza

THE

Bride of Sforza

MIRANDA SEYMOUR

HOUGHTON MIFFLIN COMPANY BOSTON

1975

cop. 1

FIRST PRINTING W

Library of Congress Cataloging in Publication Data

Seymour, Miranda.
    The bride of Sforza.

    1. Italy—History—1492–1559—Fiction.   I. Title.
PZ4.S5194Br   [PS3569.E89]   813'.5'4   74–23661
ISBN 0–395–20290–6

Printed in the United States of America

The Bride of Sforza

The house of SFORZA

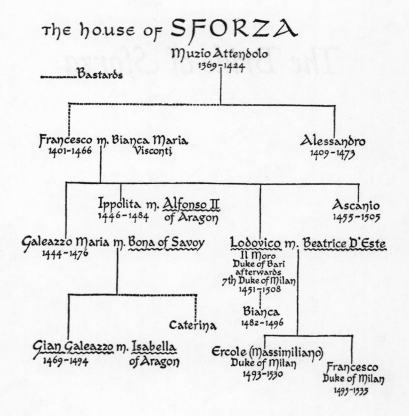

Muzio Attendolo
1369-1424

---------- Bastards

Francesco m. Bianca Maria
1401-1466   Visconti

Alessandro
1409-1473

Ippolita m. Alfonso II
1446-1484   of Aragon

Ascanio
1455-1505

Galeazzo Maria m. Bona of Savoy
1444-1476

Lodovico m. Beatrice D'Este
Il Moro
Duke of Bari
afterwards
7th Duke of Milan
1451-1508

Caterina

Bianca
1482-1496

Gian Galeazzo m. Isabella
1469-1494   of Aragon

Ercole (Massimiliano)
Duke of Milan
1493-1530

Francesco
Duke of Milan
1495-1535

The House of ESTE

Niccolò
1384–1481

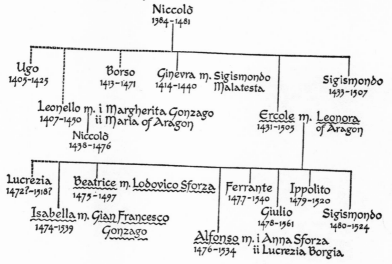

Ugo
1405–1425

Borso
1413–1471

Ginevra m. Sigismondo
1414–1440   Malatesta

Sigismondo
1433–1507

Leonello m. i Margherita Gonzago
1407–1450   ii Maria of Aragon

Niccolò
1438–1476

Ercole m. Leonora
1431–1505   of Aragon

Lucrezia
1472?–1518?

Beatrice m. Lodovico Sforza
1475–1497

Ferrante
1477–1540

Ippolito
1479–1520

Isabella m. Gian Francesco
1474–1539   Gonzago

Giulio
1478–1561

Sigismondo
1480–1524

Alfonso m. i Anna Sforza
1476–1534   ii Lucrezia Borgia

The House of ARAGON

Alfonso V of Aragon (Alfonso I of Naples)
1385–1458

Ferdinand I (Ferrante)
1424–1494

Alfonso II m. Ippolita Sforza
1448–1495

Leonora m. Ercole D'Este
1455–1494

Federigo
1450?–1504

Beatrice m. Lodovico
1475–1497   Sforza

Ferdinand II
(Ferrantino)
1468–1496

Isabella m. Gian Galeazzo Sforza
1471–1524

CHAPTER I

"WHY DO YOU WEEP, Caterina?" she said, knowing the reason. We had come home at last from the long years only to find that memory and loneliness had hidden the truth. This past, too, was dead.

Not a stone remained. Only the orange trees that had flowered every summer under my bedroom window at Maggiare dropped their dead flowers on the grass.

They had burnt the castle to the ground after my father died in 1485. King Ferrante had no use for it and his soldiers looted every corner of the castle before they set fire to it. All the books, the paintings, the tapestries, marbles and manuscripts, all gone. They say you could see Maggiare burning from the docks of Naples ten miles away.

I dream of it sometimes and then I think I am a child again, hiding behind one of the arches in the shade of the cloisters, playing *palla* with my brother Mario and Joffre, my father's page, or lying on the hot stone of the horse block, watching them at the tilts in the courtyard. I remember us as we sat on the wooden balcony that my father had constructed overlooking the garden, and my room seems to be full of the sharp scent of orange blossom. The picture never changes. I see my mother, leaning back into the shadows, watching the gulls streaming up into the hills from the sea, then I see my father, his food forgotten as he tries to interest Mario in affairs of state and the news brought back by his friends from Florence and Rome. But Mario never listened.

"There are better things in life than politics," he always said behind my father's back, so he nodded wisely at Father's words, and went on eating. I peered through the wooden pilasters until I could see Joffre, sprawled in the long grass with his back against a peach tree, his eyes half-shut against the bright sun, and his long fingers spread over the lute strings:

> "We'll laugh the heavy hours away
> In sport and love until the day has gone,
> For joy may never come again
> And we may sorrow in the dawn."

My father always said it was too sad a song and asked him to sing us another that would make us laugh. And Joffre would smile and change the rhythm to an insidious lilt as he began to sing one of the Naples street songs to bring a blush to my mother's pale cheeks and a loud excited laugh from Mario, who leaned over the balcony to hear the words more clearly.

But those days are gone forever, and when I wake up and the room is dark, I cry because only the bitterness remains.

I was born in 1475, four years after my brother Mario. I never knew my two little sisters — they died at birth. My first nurse, who had at one time looked after the little Princess Isabella of Aragon, had picked up the Spanish ways of the court. She called me Catya — it was the only concession to our foreign overlords that my father allowed at Maggiare.

Our family had not grown rich on pillaging and wars, as had many of our neighbours. My grandfather, Giovanni Vitelli, was a shrewd merchant who profited by his friendship with Cosimo de Medici, the ruler of Florence at that time. His advice and the active part he played in building up the Medici bank were generously rewarded by Cosimo. Maggiare was built on Medici money and my grandfather filled the castle with the strange and beautiful treasures that I still remember as if I touched them with my hand.

My father, the only surviving son, was brought up at Maggiare, and he loved it with a proud and fierce passion, as did we, his children. We would have died for it, but it does no good to remember such things now, too late. My mother's beauty and discrimination brought poets and painters to the castle, my father's natural kindness and generosity made all passers-by welcome to his home. Maggiare was always a place of light and laughter. I remember the sounds so clearly. Half-shutting my eyes, I hear the dancing, the clear rising notes of a hunting horn, the rippling echo of a lute through the cloisters, the soft murmuring voices of my mother and her friends as they sat in the shadow of the trees, reading love poems, remembering the past.

Yet, even as a child, a plaything fashioned out of love and lessons, with a new dress every day, I knew that all was not as it seemed. A shadow hung over the land.

In Florence, Rome and Naples, in Venice and Milan, the princes built their palaces to play in and churches so that the people could pray for them. They longed for immortality and made gods of themselves in their lifetimes. Like the emperors of imperial Rome, they sent out their agents to bring back the treasures of every land. Wise men came from Greece and the East, from the sombre Spanish courts of Ferdinand and Isabella, from Louis XI and Richard III of England, to the country where wisdom was counted as a jewel above price and a woman was more prized for her intelligence and wit than for her beauty. Nothing was beyond man's ambition, the philosophers taught us. The grandfathers of our princes had proved that. Francesco

Sforza had risen from being a brilliant *condottiere* to become the uncrowned Duke of Milan, Cosimo de Medici had built up one of the greatest banks in the world and ruled Florence with as much grace and less extravagance than his grandson Lorenzo, my father's friend. My father remembered Alfonso of Naples as the wisest ruler our kingdom had ever known. Alfonso was a Spaniard, but he knew how to make the people of Naples love him. They remembered him as Alfonso the pious, the magnanimous and the merciful.

Ambition always bears two faces. Power made many of our princes treacherous and greedy. They would offer peace and gifts with one hand while with the other they pillaged and murdered. The reverence they inspired made them intolerant of advice, and they ended by suffering for their pride and their thirst for land. Our Este relations had a bitter fight to keep Ferrara from the acquisitive hands of the Pope's nephew, Girolamo Riario, who had already assisted in the Pazzi plot to kill Lorenzo de Medici. Ferrara was saved, but Riario's ambitious plans ended in his own assassination. In Milan, the tyrannical rule of Francesco Sforza's eldest son, Galeazzo Maria, was brought to an end by his enemies, who killed the Duke while he was at his prayers. Even this, people said, would not save him from Hell.

One fear kept our princes and prelates in an uneasy alliance — the propect of an invasion of Italy. Our land was too rich and accessible not to be coveted. The man who took help from the Turk or the Frenchman against his neighbour was often the victim of his own treachery, and the foreigners watched and waited for opportunities to seize the whole. Their claims were not forgotten. Against the threat of common loss, the five states and their satellites became one city, one nation, hiding behind the all too penetrable fortress of the Alps.

These were the problems of our country, of which I understood but little, although I heard much. The fears of our own kingdom were seldom mentioned, but the unspoken was always present.

Ferrante, King Alfonso's bastard son, was not loved by his people. To all of us, Ferrante was known as the Spaniard. We would have been ashamed to call him an Italian. When he first came to the throne, some twenty years before I was born, my father and his friends had fought to keep the power that had been theirs. After four years, they were defeated by the King and seemed to be forgiven. The rule of the tyrant began and our kingdom was drained to make him glorious. When we went to Naples, the feeling of discontent and fear was evident, even to a child. No man raised his head to wave or smile as we rode across the sloping fields, the women pulled their children back into the shadows and turned their heads away. They were afraid of the King's informers. Every peasant family had suffered Ferrante's demands, given him the corn that it had taken them so long to till and reap, bought the wine that the King had robbed from their neighbours to sell back at an enforced profit, and year by year the land grew poorer, the people more beaten.

My father was bitter in his comparison of Naples to the other cities of Italy. Naples had no princely palaces other than the King's, only the dark walled fortresses where bridges and barred windows mattered more than silk hangings. But I only saw the rainbow colours of the street processions and wondered at the grey faces of the people.

The King did not forget his barons. My father had not asked to be made a marquis. Ferrante had bestowed the title anyway and had taken his dues. The fortune my grandfather had made was drained slowly into the King's coffers and the crowds of guests who had once filled Maggiare began to melt away. I was not fully conscious of the change until we went to Ferrara to stay with my mother's family. I noticed for the first time how simply my mother was dressed, how few jewels she wore in comparison to the Duchess Leonora. Their elder daughter, Isabella, mocked Mario and me for our shabby clothes and southern accents, but her little sister Beatrice, as round and merry as her sister was slim and vicious, defended us with kind words and courtesy. I remembered and loved her for it.

It was the week before my tenth birthday when everything changed, the day Joffre rode back from Naples without my father.

The sun was hot, the air heavy. I sat at my mother's feet in the courtyard, watching her comb her long, brown hair over a flat straw hat to bleach in the sun. I started to pick daisies from between the stones to plait them for her crown. There was no sound, only the wind whining through the hill grass, the trickle of water running over the parched stones down in the valley.

My mother was always laughing, playing games with me, or telling me stories of her own childhood in Ferrara, but that afternoon she was silent, and her hands lay still on the needlework in her lap.

"What are you thinking of?" I asked as I looped the daisy crown over her hat. She smiled. My father always said that she looked like the Cossa Madonna in the chapel when she smiled with sad eyes.

"I wish he had not gone to the banquet. I asked Signor Filippo if the stars were propitious this morning, and he would tell me nothing."

"Perhaps there was nothing to see."

My mother shook her head. "He said that the conjunction of Mars and Saturn was hard to decipher, but I know he saw something, for he was pale and his hands were trembling. But what he saw, I do not know."

I tried to imagine the stout astrologer pale and trembling,

and I failed. "Joffre made up a rhyme about him. 'If Signor Filippo were as tall as he is broad . . .'" I stopped. She wasn't listening. "Mother, why did the King invite my father and his friends, if he was so angry with them? Mario said that they should not have gone because the King tells lies and will do no good to his barons. Is that why you are so worried?"

"Perhaps. Giuliano is too long in returning and I do not trust King Ferrante. You remember when Signor Pontano visited us last week? I do not care for his manner, but I believe he means us no harm, and he is very close to the King. He took me on one side after dinner and suggested that we leave Maggiare for a while and go to visit the Estes at Ferrara. I asked him why, and he answered that the King is still uneasy about the power of his lords. He told me that Ferrante has had a museum made for the bodies of his enemies and that every night he goes there alone, to sit with the dead."

I shivered. "Did you tell my father this?"

"He laughed and told me to pay no heed to Pontano's nonsense. And now he has gone, and I fear for his life." She bent her head until her face was hidden in the shadow of her hat and I could not read her expression. I tried to think of something else for her.

"May we have a tournament for my birthday next week, like the one we went to see in Naples last year?"

Laughing, she smoothed my hair. "Whose idea was that, yours or Mario's?"

"Both of us," I said untruthfully, for it was Mario and Joffre who had made me promise to ask.

"If we do as you ask, who will you choose for your knight, Caterina? Not Mario, although I am sure he has offered his services, but your own chevalier to serve you and fight in your name."

I thought and thought. Galeazzo Filarte, the astrologer's son, was too ugly. Joffre would not qualify because he was only a page, and although he looked as romantic and chivalrous as Roland or Oliver, I had seen him at the tilts too many times. To be fought for by a knight who fell off in the first round would be humiliating.

My mother broke into my thoughts, to my relief. "Where is Mario? I was expecting to see him at the tilts an hour or more ago."

"I haven't seen him this afternoon. Perhaps he went hawking," I said, hoping that God would not strike me dead for such a wicked lie. But Mario had given me a red gold cross for my silence. I knew where he was. Every afternoon it was the same. Cecilia Fogliano, the daughter of my mother's waiting woman, came to his room in the west tower, to play chess, Mario said. I had listened at the door once, and almost fallen into the room when Cecilia came out with her bodice half-unlaced and her black hair hanging loose to her waist. Her face and throat were all red and she had looked so angry when she saw me that I was frightened and ran away down the stairs. She never mentioned it again, but the next day Mario had given me the cross and I no longer believed that they spent their afternoons together playing chess.

My mother held my face up towards her. "You are not a good liar, Caterina, although I admire your loyalty to Mario." She was going to question me further when the pounding of hooves on the hill brought her from her chair, straining for the sound.

"One horseman, riding fast. I am afraid, Catya."

We stood and listened. The sun had fallen behind the east tower and I felt my mother tremble as the cold shadows leapt the length of the yard. The ground vibrated to the thud of iron on turf as the rider gained the hilltop. The great wooden gates shuddered open and Joffre halted under the arch, thin and black against the sky. I would have run forward, but my mother held me still while he slowly dismounted and walked toward us, soft-footed on the stone.

"What news of my lord? Does he follow behind?" Her voice was gentle, but her hand crushed mine until the knuckles cracked.

Joffre raised his head — pale as death — and his eyes stared beyond us. His left hand was red with blood, which flowed from under his sleeve in thin rivulets, but he seemed unconscious of it. "It was a trick," he said at last. "They were murdered, every one of them, as they sat unarmed and in their cups. The wine was drugged and the King had his soldiers hidden behind the arrases to wait for the signal.

"At first all seemed well. He smiled and joked and clapped them on the shoulders, saying that he was their friend and defender. And they believed him. Like lambs to the slaughter they went. For two hours or more Ferrante and his son sat with them, calling for more drink and seeming so anxious to make amends that the lords forgot their rancour and suffered their swords to be taken from them. 'No arms among friends,' said Ferrante and still he smiled.

"And then he called for music. That must have been the signal, for the arrases were torn aside and a hundred or more men burst into the hall. There were ten soldiers to each man, my lady; they had no chance, no hope of escape. My lord fought three of them off with his bare hands, but I saw another creeping from under the table to stab at his back. I called out to him to look behind and as he turned a little weasel-faced man, may God rot his soul, came at him from the front and drove his sword through his chest up to the hilt. I ran up then and tried to pull it out, but it was stuck firm. I could do nothing, only hold his head and try to staunch the blood. He died bravely, my lady, and I think he sought to speak of you, but the blood was thick in his throat. I was still kneeling by him when I heard the King's son call out to the soldiers, asking if there were any still alive. I dropped my sword and lay still on the ground beside my lord. All around me, I could hear the soldiers moving, kicking the corpses for a sign of life. When they had satisfied themselves on that score, they threw me with the rest on a wooden cart, piled like plague victims. No guard was kept; the soldiers went back to finish the wine from the cups of the dead. I tried to find his body, but it was buried too deep and I heard the men coming back, so I crept out from the rear and hid in the shadows, near where the horses were tethered. Oh, but I would to God it had been my lord who escaped their swords, not I!" Joffre choked and stopped. Not a sound now, only the heavy silence. In the cold twilight nothing moved.

I can find no meaning in the word dead. It hangs over the head of my great, laughing father, and means nothing.

"We must leave, my lady," Joffre said gently. "Your lives are in great danger now, for Ferrante has sworn that he will not rest until he has destroyed every noble family in the kingdom."

"Leave me," my mother said. "I would be alone."

Joffre put out his hand uncertainly towards her, then drew it back and walked slowly away into the shadows.

"You also, Caterina, will go now."

"I will stay with you."

"Go!" she repeated, and her voice cracked with sorrow.

I turned as I reached the corner of the arcade, but she still stood, staring ahead. Only her hands moved, twisting in the silk of her skirt.

I picked up my heavy skirts and fled up the broad stairs, my feet clattering and echoing on the stone. I tripped and fell at the foot of a sad-faced marble naiad, brought back from

Venice for my father as a gift from Poliziano, Lorenzo de Medici's agent. Her blind gaze seemed to mock me as I lay weeping on the steps.

"Caterina, Caterina, why so many tears? Come with me, and I'll sing you a song of the sea to wash them all away." I raised my head from my arms and looked up into the kind, ugly face of Tristano d'Arengo, Mario's tutor and self-styled court poet. More than anybody else, Tristano would have known how I felt and made me understand how to bear the pain, but I could not say the words. In a curious way I felt that once I had said, "My father is dead," it would become an irrevocable truth, but until then it might only be a nightmare, a mirage.

"My mother has forbidden the tournament for my birthday," I said, and watched Tristano's face grow sad and dispirited. He took his hand away from my shoulder and sat down beside me on the step.

"And that is the cause of all this sorrow? Listen to me, little Niobe. When you are older you will weep for many things, and most of all for love. You will weep when you find it, when you have it, and when it has gone. When you have reached my age you will have shed enough tears to fill the whole Bay of Naples, and all to no purpose. But to weep because you cannot have a tournament, what would your father think of that?" He laughed and looked at me. "When you are two years older you will have men fighting for you in earnest. Wait until then to start crying."

"You don't understand," I said flatly, knowing that I was being unjust in expecting him to have seen the truth behind the lie, and I ran on up the stairs.

Mario would know what to do, I thought, as I burst into the great hall, where the laughing crowd had already begun to gather for the evening's entertainment. They were as usual too busy copying the new witticisms and fashions set by the great courts of Lorenzo de Medici and the Duke of Milan to do more than look down as I pushed my way through the rustling silks and velvets. A sudden fury brought me to a halt. It seemed vile that they should laugh and chatter away their empty existence while my father lay dead. I turned back while my hand was on the door.

"My father is dead," I said, and my voice sounded oddly high in the sudden silence.

"Are you playing one of your games, Caterina?" somebody called from the far end of the hall. They snatched at the remark as at a straw in the current. "A game, a game," they sighed with relief. One of them started to laugh.

"My father is dead," I repeated, and went through the door into the west tower.

There was no answer when I knocked at Mario's door. I opened it gently. The room was almost dark. I did not see them at first. The sounds stopped me at the door. A sobbing, rustling, flying, dying of noise, which made my legs quake so that I had to cling to the door for support. Words so soft that they seemed to brush the air — "now, here . . . you, love, I love, no, I love, my love, I am drowning, deep, now, now, oh yes, yes," to a screaming, weeping wail as I saw my brother trapped between the pale legs of Cecilia Fogliano, with his face buried in her long, black hair.

The door was half-open behind me and I knew that I could still escape without being seen, but instead I stood and stared at the heaving tangle on the bed as they strained in such a fury that I could see the muscles quivering and swelling in Mario's dark thighs, the bloody crescents on his back where Cecilia had driven her nails through the skin. Now she screamed and reared towards him with a high sobbing cry that sent me two steps back towards the door as she shook him off, sank back.

I had never seen Cecilia naked before. She looked so ugly now, with her small breasts squashed and slack, her head lolling back like a stuffed puppet as she lay with her legs spread wide across the bed. And, as I watched her mouth curving into a small smile, she opened her eyes and looked up straight into mine.

"You must forget what you have seen, Catya," Mario said as we sat side by side on the crumpled bed after Cecilia had gone, fled like a scalded cat down the stairs in a storm of silk skirts.

"How can I forget?" I wept. "It was so disgusting, so horrible, like animals."

Mario smiled. "None of those things, little sister. But you still have not explained why you are here."

It was quiet in the room when I finished speaking. Mario stood with his back to me, gazing out of the window.

"What shall we do?" I asked at last. "Joffre said we must leave Maggiare."

"Joffre's a fool. Ferrante will be watching for our next move. We're caught like rats in a trap."

"Could we write for help to Lorenzo in Florence?"

Mario sighed. "Useless. The Medici family have always been our friends, but Lorenzo would never put personal affairs before politics. He needs Naples as an ally in his plans for a peaceful Italy."

"And Duke Ercole? Our father said the Duke was like a brother to him."

"It was our father's foolish faith in man that led him to his death," Mario said bitterly. "They have good reason to call Duke Ercole 'The North Wind' and 'The Diamond' in Ferrara. He's as hard a man as Ferrante, and ambitious. It would not profit him to help us now."

"But the Duchess Leonora is kind; might not she persuade him?"

14

"No, little sister," Mario said gently. "Remember the Duchess Leonora is Ferrante's daughter."

I went to stand beside him at the window and stared down into the valley. I thought I could see helmets shining among the trees, but it was only the silver olive leaves blown back by the wind.

CHAPTER II

FOR TWELVE DAYS we waited. Mario was proved right. Our mother wrote to Ferrara, asking for any help that they might be able to give us. Ercole d'Este sent back a long letter, expressing his deepest sympathy with her loss and suggesting that we should come to Ferrara "in happier times." But there was no offer of help. Lorenzo, too, was more generous with his sorrow than with soldiers. We would be welcome in Florence, he said, but he could not afford to risk his city by antagonising Ferrante. My mother wept then, for Lorenzo had been one of my father's closest friends since childhood, and she had been certain that he would support us.

The castle seemed very empty now. The last courtiers had drifted away, back to Venice, Rome, Naples, Milan — wherever there was promise of an easy life and security. Maggiare held no more for them, and in the early hours of the morning, when the sun lay low in the sky, they rode away down the hill, chattering like starlings and never looking back to where we stood watching at the gate.

As always, those we had always taken for granted were those that stayed, but now we recognised the strength in their quietness. Tristano and Joffre and a few others worked night and day on the best methods of defence. Even I was beginning to learn something of the mechanics of war. Mario showed my mother and me how to load the great cannon when it had been rolled into position in the courtyard, its empty snout turned to the gate. Nothing was left undone. Trenches and man-traps skirted the castle walls, great bronze cauldrons were carried up to the turrets, while the kitchens were kept busier heating oil than meals, and in the great hall the long swords lay in rows on the trestle tables, their blades greased and polished. We were ready.

When she and I were alone, my mother kept up our spirits with stories of her Milanese cousin, dead ten years ago, who had proved that a woman can fight as well as any man. Bianca Maria Visconti had married the *condottiere* duke, Francesco Sforza, the father of Lord Lodovico of Milan. She had been a frail, gentle lady whose time had been devoted to feeding and clothing the poor of Milan when she was not supervising the education of her children. Yet on two occasions when there had been uprisings in Lombardy in her husband's absence, the young Duchess of Milan had worn the armour of a man and had ridden to war at the head of the Milanese troops. My favourite of the two stories was the one of her arrival without warning at a rebel castle. This gave the warlords such a shock that they dropped their weapons and surrendered on the spot.

"And so the troops from Naples will surrender when they see you," I said.

"Perhaps," my mother said, to share an illusion in which neither of us believed.

Every day Mario and Squarcia, the captain of my father's troops — what was left of them — watched from the east tower, peering down into the river valley for the scarlet sashes and the high helmets of Ferrante's men. Never a sign.

Every day I went with my mother at midday to pray in the chapel for our safety, not daring to move although my knees grew bruised and numb on the stone floor as the sun sank in gold streaks on the walls. My mother seemed already dead, so still she was as she murmured into the cold web of her hands.

Nobody would answer my questions; a shrug or a sigh was enough. What if we surrender? How many men will they send? What will they do to us? Nobody knew.

Seven days had passed. We sat in the hall, watching the space and listening for sounds that were never there.

"Now," Tristano said, the only one of us who cared to break the silence, "since today is Caterina's birthday and nobody appears to have remembered such an important fact, I think we should give up the afternoon to amuse her."

"Amusement is for those who cannot think," Mario said slowly, sliding his hand down one of the shafts of the polished swords. My father's death had made a man of my fourteen-year-old brother.

"We have too much time for thought," Tristano answered, and he picked me up from my chair and stood me on the table.

I had forgotten all about my birthday, although the week before I had thought of nothing else. It didn't seem to matter much anymore and I stood silently, not knowing what to do. Tristano bent over the table and whispered, "Choose a game, any game you like. It will take their minds from worry for an hour or two."

"Yes," I said, and forced myself to smile and be a child again.

"As your queen," I proclaimed grandly, striking a pose with my feet astride the crossed swords, "I command that you shall seek me out in whatever place I choose to hide."

"Excellent!" Tristano said, and clapped me on the shoulders with such vigour that I almost fell over. "We will come and hunt you out after counting to a hundred."

"Hush!" Mario said suddenly. "Did you hear?"

We listened. Nothing. Stillness. Mario shrugged and sank

back, looking so old, so tired that I reached out to touch him. He patted me with my father's hand and smiled.

"I'm sorry to spoil your game, little sister. You run and hide."

I looked round at the door once to make sure that they were not cheating and watching me. Sitting in the half light with their hands covering their faces, still as saints waiting to be martyrs. Only Mario kept one hand on the table, loosely clasped round a dagger's hilt.

None of the old favourite hiding places pleased me that afternoon, although I stopped and looked at each of them from habit. The longer I could remain hidden, I thought, the less time there would be for evening prayers in the chapel, and so I wandered on up the stone steps past the tapestries on the walls to the long low rooms under the roof.

I had always meant to explore them, but this was the first time that I had done more than peer from the safety of the arch at the top of the stairs. The uneven floors were hidden under a blanket of dust that rose in clouds to choke me as I walked forward. Chests and coffers, tables and books were stacked in great blocks up to the rafters. A bat, frightened from sleep by my footsteps, flew at me from the shadows. I ducked away from his jagged wings and ran on.

A distant clatter on stone sent me scurrying in a sudden panic across the room in search of a hiding place. I had not expected them to follow me so quickly. A great chest of age-black wood, jutting square across the room, blocked my passage. Its panelled front was carved with the heads of devils and grotesques that I had seen peering down from church gutters, but these had been fashioned by such a craftsman that even their wooden hair seemed to writhe like snakes. Their eyes had been cut with such detail that the pupils seemed to spring clear of their sockets to stare on stalks, and the whole chest let out a curious, heavy smell, like dead flowers or weeds on stagnant water.

I turned to look for a friendlier hiding place, but time and the grim prospect of the chapel changed my mind. I heaved up the heavy lid and clambered in, using the devils' heads as steps. The smell that I had already noticed was almost overpowering inside the chest. I coughed and spluttered, trying to raise the lid enough to let in a fraction of light and air. I pushed with all the strength of fear. It would not budge. The clasp must have caught. I was trapped.

God knows how many hours I must have lain there, weeping with fright when my screams and hammerings on the side of the chest brought nobody. Silence was my only answer and I began to wonder what would happen if no one found me. Perhaps they would not think of looking in the attics. I would slowly starve to death. Tristano had once told me a story . . . I tried not to think about it, but there is no better way to remember than to try to forget. There had been a girl, very young, very beautiful, who had hidden in a chest on her wedding day and never been found. Only the bones and a few scraps of rotting silk were left when the chest was opened at last. My sobs choked and broke in the dust of the dark as I started to beat again at the heavy wood.

I stopped at the sound of feet running up the stairs, unable to decide whether to give in and be caught or risk remaining in my coffin forever. Pride lost, and I started to call and shout.

The lid opened suddenly and I sighed with relief.

"Thank heaven you came! I was so frightened! Why did you take so long?"

I looked up and stopped short. It was no face that I had seen before. In the shadowing wings of the helmet only his mouth was visible, twisted into a smile by a long scar that drew the side of his lip upwards. He stared down in surprise for a moment and then the artificial smile broke into a loose, stupid grin as he scooped me up and held me to the light.

"Put me down at once!" I said, terror turning a plea into a command, but he only laughed and began to pull at the laces of my black bodice.

I thought of Cecilia writhing under Mario and screamed. The smell of blood was strong on the hand he clamped over my mouth.

"Stay quiet and you'll stay alive. Or do you want to service the rest of the troops?"

"How dare you! Do you realise who I am?" My voice trembled and the words sounded empty and ridiculous.

"You're doing better than the rest of your family, cursed be their names!" he said and spat, very deliberately. I watched the saliva trickle across my arm.

"What do you mean? Where is my mother? Mario? Take me to them."

"You can join them in time, although I wouldn't be so eager if I were you," he said and swore as the knotted laces over my breast resisted his fingers.

"Stop," I said uncertainly. His weight dropped on me, his hands felt my legs, my eyes closed and I remembered Cecilia again.

"Really, Giovanni, do you think of nothing else? Get up, you great lout. There'll be time enough for that later."

My body was light as my captor jumped up as though he had been hit. In the doorway above a tall, thin man stood leaning against the left pillar with his arms crossed over his chest.

"Who's the girl?"

"One of the family, Captain. The daughter, I suppose."

"Poor child," said the Captain, looking down at me. "Too

good for your thumbs, Giovanni." He bent down until the scarlet feathers in his helmet brushed against my face. "What's your name? Why weren't you down with the rest of your family?"

I stared silently at him, trying to pull the laces of my dress together. He saw the movement and looked away politely.

"She *is* one of the Vitellis all right," he said in an undertone to the soldier. "Serving girls don't worry about propriety."

"What are you going to do with her?" asked the sullen Giovanni.

"I think we'll take her back with us to Naples. We can't leave her here."

"Why not, the stupid cow! She should go the same way as the rest of them."

"I think that is for me to decide," the Captain said, and I looked up, startled by the sudden coldness of his voice.

"For the King to decide, you mean."

"Your Romagna manners stink as usual. I will have no peasant insolence in my ranks, as I have told you before."

Giovanni shrugged in anger and swung away from the window to the steps, his spurs rebellious on the treads.

The Captain sighed and held out his hands towards me in a gesture of mock despair. "I'm sorry," he said. "I wish you had another name." I nodded and followed him slowly down the stairs. So quiet, too quiet. No sign of life, not a whisper, not a mutter, only the circling echo of footsteps. As we reached the bottom the Captain turned and put his arm across to bar my way.

"How brave are you?"

"My father was the bravest man in Naples, sir. He taught me courage."

"I met your father once," he said. "He was too wise to die in such a way. If you have some of his courage, I will walk with you. If you fear what you will see, I will take you from here by another way."

"What do you mean? We will go the way I always go, through the hall to the courtyard. I'm not afraid of your soldiers."

"You have no need to be, Caterina. You misunderstand me."

"How do you know my name?"

He looked back at me, and his face was sad. "Your mother called for you."

I pounced on his words. "Then she *is* here still?" He had walked on ahead and did not hear me. The hall was empty. Only the swords lay scattered on the floor, gleaming dull, blood-rusted.

I could hardly recognise the courtyard. The gutters by the cloisters ran scarlet to stain the cobbles; bodies sprawled like bacchantes everywhere. Heads lolled back to stare empty-eyed at the sky; puppet legs spread on the stone. The cannon lay squat and still, pointing at the clouds. The smell of blood and smoke was very strong. I forgot the Captain, who stood back silently to let me pass.

I didn't know what dead men looked like before. Tristano and Joffre, lying together with their faces turned to the sun. So still in death. I followed their eyes up to the old iron cage above the portcullis, once used to punish traitors but empty for as long as I could remember. It was occupied now. A body lay across it, half-thrust through the wire door so that the legs hung loose in the air.

"You brother," said the Captain. A hundred miles away I heard my voice, no longer mine, asking for my mother. "Is she dead?"

He nodded, his face impassive, and pointed to the corner under the east tower, where shadows made a heavy jumble of the shapes. I walked slowly, knowing what I would see. Only the crumpled pile of red silk to know her body from those of

the Foglianos, mother and daughter, their three heads lying
in a trinity, three corpses piled apart. Only her long hair
stretched over the cobbles to make my mother's body still one
piece. I picked up the red silk and hid her head. I wanted
to cry, but my eyes were dry as dead leaves. I could only stand
and stare with my throat aching and throbbing.

When the Captain lifted me onto the front of his horse and
rode out under the gate in front of the silent soldiers, I sat
motionless. I did not resist and I did not understand.

CHAPTER III

I HAD NOT BEEN to Naples since the previous summer when we had come with the Duke of Salerno and his family to the festival of Saint Theresa. The city had looked so beautiful then with great rainbow arches of flowers over every street turning the puddles into coloured pools, the high bleak walls of the houses hidden behind patterned cloths of scarlet and gold with branches of olive pinned to every door. I remembered how the crowds of people jostled up against our horses and how I had laughed when my father told me that the weight of jewellery on the women was put there in order to prove they were the donkeys of rich husbands. I had thought that they must all be very grand since many of them were laden with gold charms and crosses so that they could scarcely move, although their faces showed no effort under the heavy rouge and their eyes were bright as peacocks' tails.

I wondered if perhaps the same men who now rode so stiff and grim behind the Captain had strutted among the bright caval-cades that other time, dressed like gods to awe the crowds who parted before them.

Today I would not have known it to be the same city. The streets behind the fortress walls were empty, and as we rode in single file through the narrow passages, the shutters overhead were closed when we passed by, as though caught in a gust of wind. The few groups huddled at the street corners dissolved as we approached, and the women round the wells in the piazzas stopped their gossip and drew back in tight clusters to stare at the soldiers, their arms folded across their bodices as though to protect themselves.

"Are you taking me to see the King?" I asked as we broke away from the main route to the palace into a side street.

The Captain shook his head. "The first public audience is tomorrow morning. I would gladly offer you a bed with my own children for the night, but as the King's prisoner you must sleep in the Castel dell'Ovo."

I stared at him in horror. "The prison?"

"Your family are declared traitors, Caterina. If I housed you, I would be a traitor's confederate. The risk is too great. I, too, have a family."

In my terror I forgot the pride of the Vitellis and begged and pleaded, but the Captain rode on without listening.

The Castel dell'Ovo had been used to terrify Mario and me when we were very young. Whenever we had done anything wrong, my mother would threaten us with the Castel, saying that all wicked children were sent there until they had learned to behave better. I had grown up with a horror of the mass of granite rising before us now like a leviathan from the grey blue sea to swallow me up, and my spirits sank as the Captain nudged his horse onto the narrow causeway that led to it from the deserted sea front. The huge walls overshadowed us, chilling the stones and fretting the horses into a nervous side step.

I shivered and the Captain looked down at me, sensing my fear. "Only one night, I promise you. Tomorrow you shall see the King, and who knows what may happen?" he said as he lifted me off the pommel of the saddle.

"Who knows indeed?" I answered hopelessly and the words came back to mock me like ghosts from the castle walls.

Giovanni, who had been lurking in the rear flank of the troops, came forward to the gate to demand entrance in the King's name.

A square hole in the heavy wooden door opened like a sprung trap and a small, angry face appeared with such speed that it seemed to have been pulled into place on a wire. Startled by another big nose so close to his own, Giovanni took three steps backwards towards the edge of the causeway. I hoped he would fall over, but he balanced himself neatly, his spurred heels over the sea.

"Well, who's the poor wretch you've brought in this time?" asked the bodiless head in a high, squeaking voice.

"A young lady, signor, if you would be so very kind as to let us in," Giovanni said in an ingratiating whine. In other circumstances, I would have laughed at the contrast to the rough tone he had used on me at Maggiare.

"I wouldn't, given half the chance," the head said sharply, pushing its nose forward to sniff the troops with disgust. "It's you lot who ought to be in here for your foulness and murderings. I don't suppose she's done any harm, poor soul."

"Remember that we represent the King, signor. I don't think he would care to hear that you had spoken in this way," the Captain said sternly, but I saw him hide his smile behind his hand.

The head looked up sharply, the small, shrewd eyes sunk in mottled cheeks swivelling towards the Captain and me. "Oh, it's you," he said in a tone that made it difficult to know whether he despised or respected the Captain. His head vanished as suddenly as it had appeared and a moment later the great gate swung open. The owner of the head, a tiny man no bigger than one of my father's dwarfs, marched towards us, very dapper in his gold and scarlet uniform. He halted in front of me, so small that I could look straight over his head.

"And since when has the King ordered the imprisonment of children?"

The Captain sighed. "It's only for one night, Roberto. I will myself ensure that she has a place in the King's audience tomorrow."

"Oh, well, that's not so bad then," the keeper said in a milder voice. "You'd better leave her with me. I'll make sure that she's comfortable."

The Captain nodded and patted me on the shoulder. "I'll see that you are released as soon as possible tomorrow morning, Caterina. Roberto will look after you well. He has a soft spot for pretty young ladies."

I watched the horsemen clattering down the causeway back to Naples, talking and laughing now that their day's work was over and any guilt that they felt could be forgotten.

"Caterina, eh?" the small man said as I turned towards him. "Pretty girl, pretty name. Hey! Hey! Age?"

"Ten today, sir."

He fired comments and questions like pistol shots as we walked through the whale's mouth into the dark yard, then on into the castle's belly of passages, unevenly floored and ill lit. At the end of each row of cells, another door was locked behind us, shutting out the world. I tried to control myself, crushing my hands behind my back, but every sound added to my terror, the clanging of gates, the dull boom of waves against the castle walls and the steady drip of water falling from stone to stone.

"Here we are." He unlocked a door, letting a dusky patch of light into the passage. I shrank back against the damp wall, trapped.

"Come along, my dear. I'm a busy man." He sighed as I moved further away from him down the passage. Without hope, I began to run, knowing it was no use. He caught me easily, shook his head at me, without anger.

"Please," I whispered, "please, don't leave me alone."

He laughed. "You're a funny one! Not a word for the last ten minutes, and now you want company. I told you, miss, I've got plenty of other people to look after here. What are you so worried about? You'll be home with your family again soon enough."

"No," I said slowly, "no." And my tears rose to choke me.

I heard him whistle softly. "So that's it! Poor child!"

I could not see through the mist, but I felt him lead me forward and then sit down beside me. Beyond caring, I buried my face in my hands and sobbed while he patted me awkwardly on the back. It must have been more than an hour before I leant back, exhausted and shivering.

"I should go," the keeper said, "but before I do, I'll tell you a story to send you to sleep. Now, have you ever wondered how the Castel dell'Ovo got its name?"

I had not, but I nodded.

"Or have you ever found out?" he asked anxiously.

"No."

"Good, good," he said, and he told me the story of how Virgil had used his magical powers to balance a great castle upon a hen's egg that he had placed on the bed of the Bay of Naples. He told the story well, and I laughed weakly.

"Oh, well, I must go and do my rounds. You'll be safe now." It was a statement, not a question, and he rose briskly. I was still smiling at the story and did not fully sense that I was imprisoned until the key turned in the lock, and I heard the sound of his heels dying into a last echo.

For the first time since I had been released from the chest, I began to think of the future. It looked bleak, optimistic though I am by nature. I planned appeals I could make to the King, but none of them sounded right, and although I tried to push it to the back of my mind, one sentence of my mother's kept stubbornly coming back to me. "He told me that Ferrante has had a museum made for the bodies of his enemies and every night he goes there alone, to sit with the dead." What if that was the fate in store for me? I could imagine the scene, the King's whispers to his ministers, his finger pointing at me as he shouted: "Vitelli's daughter? To the museum with her!" I tried to tell myself that this was a nightmare, that I was being childish, but it was no use. I began to look around the room for anything that would divert my mind and noticed some letters on the wall, caught by the dusty, slanting light. Names and thoughts of other prisoners were there, poems half-finished, some so high that I had to stand on the rickety stool to read them. Many of them were people whose names meant nothing to me; Muzio Attendolo, Girolamo Schiavoni and, far above my head, one that I could hardly make out. I stood on my toes and squinted up at the uneven letters, trying to puzzle them into a name. An E, then two letters that I could not read, and another E. The name and the solution to my problems came to me with such force that I nearly fell off the stool. E — — E could only be Este, one of the relations of Beatrice, Ferrante's granddaughter.

Beatrice had come from Ferrara to visit the Naples court two years ago with her mother, the Duchess Leonora, and I remembered my father telling me that the King had been so delighted with his little granddaughter that he had begged to be allowed to keep her with him. The Duchess, as dutiful a daughter as she was a mother, had gone home, leaving Beatrice at Naples. As far as I knew she was still here, although the hostility between my father and Ferrante had made it impossible for us to meet.

Beatrice and I were nearly the same age, though I was the older by nine months, and when we had visited the Estes for a month three years ago, we had become almost like sisters. We had shared a feeling of inferiority to Isabella, Beatrice's elder sister, and our friendship was founded on the qualities that we lacked and Isabella possessed. Beatrice and I were as round as Isabella was slender and beautiful. When the Este children were asked to entertain the grownups, the applause and admiration were all for Isabella; so talented, so amusing, so perfect that Beatrice and I cordially hated her. Envy is a good base for friendship and when Beatrice and I parted, we had exchanged locks of hair and sworn eternal love through enough tears to fill a fishpond. If Beatrice were still at the court, I was sure she would do her best to help me . . . I fell asleep feeling almost happy.

I slept soundly on the hard little bed. When the keeper rapped on the barred window in the door, I stared at him in surprise, wondering if my mother had forgotten what she was doing to let a man see me in bed. Then I remembered and wished that I had not.

"Up with you, miss! The Captain's kept his promise and if you want to see the King today, you'd better hurry before they shut the doors of the audience room. Then you'll be in a pretty pickle. The next one isn't until next week."

I pulled my knees up to my chin under the rough cloth and stared at him over them in silence, waiting for him to go away. He made no attempt to move and I reluctantly started to button on my dress behind the blanket. I had never had to dress myself before and was making a very poor job of it when he began to laugh.

"First time you've done it yourself, hey? None of the ladies who come here can manage without their waiting women, although they seem to get used to it pretty soon."

"Of course I can manage," I said, struggling to fasten the three buttons just out of reach in the middle of my back. I did them up after a fashion and stood up with a smile of triumph.

The result amused him so much that he had to sit down on the stool to get his breath back.

"And you expect me to believe that you've done that before? Oh dear, the King won't think much of you if you arrive looking like that. Look and see for yourself, miss."

He produced a piece of broken glass from his pocket and held it up to reflect a scruffy creature who might be myself.

"Never mind," he said, still wheezing and hissing through his last teeth. "I'll get my wife to give you a hand. She's used to brightening the lives of some of the poor ladies here." He turned to give a shout down the passage: "Lucia, Lucheeyah!"

She was a kindly, merry little woman, even smaller than her husband, with scarlet shiny cheeks and her hair bound up on top of her head like a harvest loaf. She nodded brightly at me and went to work at once with fingers light with years of experience, pinning and coiling and twisting the snarls out of my hair. She was one of those women who like an audience but no answers, and I could not have put in a word as she slipped from one subject to another with the practised ease of a gossip. In the time it took her to dress me and to smooth my hair into a plait that hung to my waist, I had learned that she was a Lombard by birth, that her husband was a good man but stupid, "No idea of bettering himself, you understand," that her mother had come to Naples as a girl and had become a waiting woman to the ruler of Naples in my grandfather's time, the notorious Queen Giovanna, "Of whom I will say nothing," she added darkly. She then proceeded to say a great deal. I heard of the old queen's passion for her army general, Lodovico Sforza's grandfather, Muzio Attendolo.

"The same man whose name is written up there on the wall?" I asked. She nodded with disgust. "You know what his crime was? Being at the court when the queen found a new lover.

So she put him away until he could be of use to her, or so they say. These upstart kings and queens, they think they are gods, able to turn the world to their will. And as for Ferrante and the young Duke . . . How Alfonso could have spawned such a son, and he was such a good, understanding sort of man! But it's not my place to say."

I sat quiet and listened, thinking I might hear something useful, but she was well away on her pet grievance against the King. According to her, Ferrante was bankrupting all the farming families in the kingdom by buying up their stock at a cheap rate and selling it too dearly.

"The only redeeming feature he has as far as I'm concerned is his behaviour toward his grandchild. They say there's nothing he won't do to please the girl. She's a dear, sweet-natured little thing, too — it's a shame she's not old enough to influence him about some of the things that matter. But there it is. She'll be going back to be married to the Duke of Bari soon, so I've heard, and he old enough to be her father." She wagged her head happily like any gossip with a captive audience.

"Beatrice, you mean?" I said, trying to look indifferent. She stopped short and stared at me.

"You know her?"

"She's my cousin," I said.

"And she likes you?"

"We were like sisters."

"I wonder," she said, her round face creased with the effort of thinking instead of talking.

"Wonder what?" I asked. I longed for somebody to see how ingenious I was.

"How to ensure that she'll be present when you see the King. It's your best chance, if you don't want to end up buried in this hellhole. If I could get word to the princess . . . but there's so little time. We'll try it anyway. My daughter works in the castle. She could make sure a note or message was delivered, but she might need a little encouragement." She looked round nervously at the door. "Roberto will kill me if he hears of this."

She looked me over appraisingly with the shrewd gaze of a peasant and her eyes fastened on the heavy gold cross that my brother had given me. It wasn't the moment to become sentimental. I unfastened it and gave it to her.

"Perhaps your daughter would like this?"

"Gold?" she asked, weighing it in the flat of her broad, red palm.

"Yes."

"That will do well enough." She straightened up and smoothed down her skirt with the air of one who has driven a good bargain. "I'll see to it," she said, and went away down the labyrinth, shouting as she went to her husband to take me down to the gate.

CHAPTER IV

"A GOOD OMEN," the Captain said, looking up at the clear spiral of the sky where the gulls spun and sank and whirled on the suck of the wind. In the shadow of the pier the fishermen looked up from their work, dredging the bright sea grass from their nets to display their catch of mussels and oysters. The coming and going of the King's prisoners must have been a matter of indifference to them. They saw it often enough.

> *"I loved a girl, a fair one*
> *And loved her for a day*
> *We promised love forever*
> *And then I went my way,"*

the Captain sang as we rode abreast down the sea front over the neat half circles of the cobbles, and when we passed a group of girls, swinging along arm in arm to morning Mass, he swept off his plumed helmet with a great flourish, to shake its feathers to a flurry. They laughed and turned their heads away, but I saw them look back. We turned up the Via dei Armorai where the workmen were sitting in front of their shops in the slant of the sun, polishing silver breastplates and swords while they exchanged friendly insults with their neighbours.

It was a good half-hour's journey to the Castello Nuovo, but the Captain passed the time in telling me stories. I heard the legend of the Castel dell'Ovo for the second time, and then he told me of the time when Naples was still only a fishing village and the dead body of Parthenope was swept up on the shore. She had, the Captain told me, been the most beautiful of the sirens who tried to seduce Odysseus with their songs and she had drowned herself in shame because she had failed.

Tristano had told me the same story on many occasions, but then it had been a lesson. Today the Captain told it because he liked the myth and because she had been a beautiful girl.

"I shouldn't really tell you," he said as we rode up through the place of public executions, the Piazza del Mercato, "but I think you would be glad to know that the Duke of Salerno escaped from the . . . the . . ." He stopped, lost for a word to describe last week's mass slaughter of my father and his friends.

I was sorry for him. "The banquet?" I said.

"Exactly. I know he was one of your father's greatest friends and he must have had a little more wisdom, if you will forgive my saying so. He never went to the banquet and when the troops were sent in to his castle they found it empty with a message pinned to the gate, saying, 'An old sparrow does not walk into the cage.' Crafty old devil. He'd got wind of the plan and fled to France."

He laughed with me and I began to wonder how deep his loyalties to the Aragon dynasty went, but there was no time to explore that any further. The twin semicircular towers of the Castello Nuovo rose before us with the newly carved frieze of Ferrante's father, Alfonso the Good, on his triumphal entry into Naples, bridging the gap between the two towers.

As we came up to the portcullis, two guards stood aside at a word from the Captain and we rode in. The well of the courtyard was shadowed by the high walls and I shivered, suddenly afraid. There was no reason why the keeper's daughter should not have taken the cross without passing on the message.

"I must leave you now, Caterina," the Capain said softly and he bowed over my hand.

"Do you generally treat your prisoners with such courtesy, my dear Feo? It seems a trifle out of order, although admirable, no doubt."

The Captain turned and bowed stiffly to a small, exquisite man who leaned forward on his gilt and enamel stick to thrust his sharp, pointed face near mine. I moved back from the stale smell of scent and old sweat, but his thin fingers clamped over my shoulder like a rabbit trap.

"Not so fast, little miss." He looked at the Captain who stood at attention, his face expressing nothing. "Who is she, Feo? Not one of your conquests, surely. She's not pretty enough for that. No, let me see if I can solve the riddle." He raised his stick to his lips and sucked at the gold top. I noticed his nails, rimmed in black, and I wondered at the Captain's subservience.

"One of the barons' daughters! That's it," the man said, jabbing at me with the stick. "Well, Feo, right or wrong?"

"I can speak for myself," I said. "I am Caterina Vitelli."

He snatched his hand back from my shoulder and turned on the Captain. "What does this mean? I thought you had my instructions to deal with the entire family, Captain."

The Captain hesitated before speaking. "I'm prepared to face the consequences, my lord, and whatever you may say, I cannot imagine that your father will object to my bringing him a ten-year-old child."

I stared with renewed interest at the King's son, remembering the only time I had met his daughter, Isabella of Aragon. I had asked her if she loved her father and her reaction had shocked me. "Is it possible to love what we despise?" Isabella said, sitting very still with her sallow Spanish skin turning red. "I don't know," I said. "I never thought about it." "Then I cannot give you an answer," she said, and changed the subject. Seeing her father now for the first time, I understood: His appearance did not tally with the legendary accounts of his courage and skill on the battlefield. It was just another courtier who stood before me.

"Appearances can be deceptive," the King's son said, his head turned up to watch a cloud bowling out of sight over the battlements. He raised his stick again to poke at the back of a man in a friar's habit. "Here, you. Take this . . . young lady to the audience chamber."

"Yes, my lord. Of course, my lord," the friar said, looking scared out of his wits. I followed him through a double arch at the end of the courtyard. The grim exterior of the palace had given me no clue to the splendour of Ferrante's style of life. As I walked behind the friar through a maze of marble-floored passages, I stared in amazement at the great tables of alabaster, the gold vases and jars taller than a grown man, Persian and Turkish tapestries and shelves of Venetian glass, each piece fluted and twisted into shivering perfection.

In the distance I could hear voices growing from a hum to a throb as we walked on, and as the friar opened a door at the end of the passage, I clapped my hands against my ears to shut out the din.

Three broad stone steps led down into a low room of such length that I found it hard to see the other end. We were evidently at the back where the less important cases were waiting, for the floor seemed almost alive with the creep of the crippled, deformed and aged of Naples, who lay propped against the walls and each other, half covered with rags that were only kept together by their dirt. Many of them looked as if they could not move. They lay still with one hand outstretched, waiting for someone, me perhaps, to fill their palms.

The friar, immune through habit to such horrors, walked

among them, kicking out of the way any twisted limb that lay across his path. "Stinking vermin!" he threw back at me as an exorcism.

I was busy looking for Beatrice, and as we came up from the shadows towards the dais at the end of the room, I saw her standing beside Ferrante's gilded throne. She was almost hidden behind the vast bulk of the King, who sat crouched like a brooding toad, his legs spread wide under a long robe of gold cloth. Seeing him for the first time, I could not understand what had made my father trust him. The friar had come to a halt, and I was able to study the King's face at leisure.

Under his flat gold cloth cap his hair was pulled down in a fringe to his eyebrows and coasted back from his heavy face in waves. Where most men's cheeks taper in, Ferrante's swelled into bulbous jowls that overhung his collar, pulling the skin into bloodhounds' pouches. Less of a toad, more of a butcher. His small, mean eyes hurried nervously around the room and his constant smile appeared to be the fault of a spasm. It was a cruel face and a clever one. I did not find much hope for my future in it.

As I looked, Beatrice saw me and inclined her head, very slightly. She was dressed like a king's granddaughter with her long black hair braided and bound with pearls, and a necklace of heavy square-cut rubies dragged at the tender skin of her throat. They glowed like clots of blood, but there was no colour in the face above them. The cold artifice of Ferrante's court was no place for children, and I saw that it had taken Beatrice's childhood away.

She was hidden from my sight as King Ferrante rose heavily to his feet. The hall rose with him in obedience.

"Ecco il maestro," said the King, and held out his hands. There was a flurry in the crowd and a parting of bodies and I saw the round dome of Pontano's head bobbing sedately up the hall. When he reached the steps up to the dais, he bowed his head quickly and spoke to the King in an inaudible mutter. Ferrante's face darkened and the empty smile changed to a pout.

"Where is the man? We will see what he has to say," he said aloud and turned back to sit in his chair of authority.

"Giuliano Averro, come forward in the name of His Most Royal Majesty of the Kingdom of Naples," Pontano said in a low, expressionless voice that carried clearly over the murmur and shuffle of the crowd. After some pushing and prodding a small, depressed-looking man standing in front of me was poked out of hiding by his neighbours and pushed towards the throne with such energy that he arrived on his knees. Ferrante looked down at him as though a stray cur had broken his privacy, then he spoke with cold deliberation.

"Signor, we have heard that you have shown reluctance to purchase the required percentage of royal corn. Can you explain this to our satisfaction?"

Averro shifted from one foot to the other. "The corn was not ripe, Your Majesty. It was of no use to me."

"No use," Ferrante repeated, dropping the words like hot mozzarella in a pan. "No use. Do you realise who is the owner of the crop you were fortunate enough to be given the privilege of buying?" He did not wait for an answer. "I am. Did you know that, Averro?"

"Yes, Your Majesty."

"And do you still feel that you are above buying the royal corn? Is that why you are here? Perhaps you have not considered the fact that you may face a charge of treason. It is not a hard choice to make. I'm sure you are ready to see reason, now."

I could not blame the poor farmer for his answer, although

I despised him for it. I was still looking after him as he slunk back through the hall when the friar drove a sharp finger into my back.

"Get out there. They're calling your name." I wanted to move, but my legs seemed to be pillars in the floor. "Unless you want to go back to prison, that is," the friar whispered viciously. I moved then, walking slowly forward until I stood, shaking like a jelly, at the foot of the dais.

"Vitelli's daughter, Your Majesty," Pontano said and he looked at me as though I were a stranger. I stared back at him, trying to shame him into recognition, but he did not waver.

Ferrante leaned forward in his chair, then turned as Beatrice pulled at his sleeve. It was strange to see the change in his face as he bent towards her. Almost as though two men dwelt inside the same skull. I could not hear what Beatrice said, but every now and then she looked towards me with a smile. Ferrante's frown remained, but at least he was listening to her. She finished speaking and stood meekly looking down at her hands. Ferrante looked irritated and said nothing. I waited and the minutes were infinitely long.

"Well," he said at last in a voice that was far from amiable, "since Beatrice has begged for your release and offers to take you back to Ferrara with her, I suppose there is nothing I can do. Pronounce her free and bring on the next case."

The friar shook me by the shoulders. "Thank the King for his kindness, girl. Don't just stand there staring."

I muttered my thanks, but the words stuck in my throat. The King appeared satisfied. He nodded and I walked slowly back down the hall behind the friar.

As we came to the broad steps a small girl darted out from the crowd and pushed past the friar to my side.

"Here," she said, holding out her hand. "My mother gave me this, but I would rather you took it back. I was glad to be able to help." She pressed something into the palm of my hand and disappeared as swiftly as she had come. I looked down. It was my gold cross.

CHAPTER V

THERE WERE TEARS and promises and presents on the day before our departure to Ferrara. Beatrice had been a favourite at the Naples court. One scene remained in my mind afterwards.

"You know my cousin Bella?" Beatrice asked as we sat together in her room, drinking Malaga wine with a dish of larks.

"Isabella of Aragon? I met her once."

"You liked her?"

I shrugged. "You make it an accusation. We only talked for a few minutes. She seemed very unhappy."

"Perhaps she is. With a father like Alfonso . . . I never thought of that before. I only knew that she was a very depressing companion." Beatrice sipped at her wine thoughtfully. "I heard yesterday that she is to be married to the Duke of Milan, and I thought it would be amusing to find out whether she knows the stories about him."

"Why? What stories?" I started to nibble a Savoy biscuit, disinclined to move.

"I'll tell you later. Come!" Beatrice said imperiously. I followed her out of the room.

We found her cousin reading in a sunny corner of the long gallery. I watched the two girls exchange kisses, and heard from the pitch and sweetness of their voices that they had little affection for each other. In appearance, they were very dissimilar. Isabella of Aragon was a tall girl, thin rather than slim, with heavy lidded eyes that accentuated the mournfulness of her face. Her black hair was sleekly coiled into two shells over her ears, her dress of slashed orange silk drew attention to the sallowness of her skin. And yet there was a sweetness and grace about her that I was bound to admit that Beatrice lacked. Had she not been her father's daughter, I could have liked her.

"When do you come north for the marriage, Bella?" asked Beatrice, her eyes wide and innocent.

"In two years, I believe," Isabella of Aragon said. "I long to meet him."

"Oh, you have not met him! How very odd!" Beatrice smiled. "Well, I hope you will not forget me when you are Duchess of Milan. I shall feel a poor creature in comparison."

"I doubt that," Bella said dryly. She looked as if she wished to end the conversation, but Beatrice sat down beside her.

"Now, why do you suppose that none of us have met Gian! Does it worry you, Bella? After all, we have all heard of his uncle Lodovico, but nobody talks of Gian."

Bella stood up and moved away from the window. "I do not know what you are trying to say, Beatrice, but I think you should stop listening to court gossip."

Beatrice sighed. "I was only curious, and now I have hurt your feelings. Poor Bella, you should not take offense so easily."

"Oh, nothing you say can worry me, I promise you that," Bella said, but her cheeks were red with anger.

"Then we part as friends?"

"Naturally."

Beatrice hummed to herself as we walked back down the passage, running her hand along the glass vases to leave a chiming echo behind us.

"Is there something wrong with Gian?" I asked.

"I'll tell you about it one day," Beatrice said. "Poor Bella! They never even told her. I could almost pity her."

We took the sea road out of Naples. It was a soft, warm morning with the wind plucking gently at our thin veils. Everybody was glad to be going home to Ferrara. They were tired of the sullen atmosphere of Ferrante's court. Even the horses sensed it and trotted briskly uphill, their noses turned into the wind. One of the pages began to sing and the ladies were laughing and chattering like sparrows. My spirits lifted as we left the low hills behind us and I turned to smile at Beatrice.

"That's the first time I've seen you look happy," she said. "You must be feeling recovered."

I felt guilty at once, but it was hard to remain sad in her company. Her joy in life was so infectious. Everything delighted her. She glanced behind her as we came down the hill into a long, flat stretch, and smiled with satisfaction. Nobody was watching us.

"I'll race you to the next hill, Catya." She dug her heels in as she spoke. We flew like birds down the open stretch and my tight plaits uncoiled and whipped across my face as I held my head up to the snap and bite of the wind. My palfrey snorted disapprovingly, unused to such vulgar speed. She lacked any spirit of competition and my shouts and kicks had no effect at all. Beatrice was waiting under the trees as I came up to join her at a placid trot.

"That took you a long time. I've been waiting for at least five minutes."

"Your horse is faster, that's all."

"I'm a better rider, you mean."

"You started before me."

Beatrice burst out laughing.

"You're a worse loser than Isabella, and I never would have thought that possible."

"How is she?" I asked, more from politeness than interest.

Beatrice hesitated before answering. "Where are the others?"
I looked back down the track where dust still swirled up from
the horse's hooves.

"Half a mile behind, at least."

We rode slowly on while Beatrice talked, her voice flat and
even, emotionless. "Isabella," she said, and paused. "I can't
bear to have her as a sister. She . . . she likes to excel in
everything, and she does. She recites pages of Livy and Virgil,
she can dance better than anyone else, she sings beautifully, she
cares for nobody but herself, and everybody loves her except me
and I am only her shadow."

She turned in the saddle to look at me. "Have I shocked you,
Catya? I know that you and Mario were very close to each
other . . ."

"Don't," I said, but the cage over the castle gate was already
in my mind, creaking under the new weight within it.

Beatrice looked at me and shrugged. "I have learnt one lesson
in Naples," she said. "Never show your feelings. My grandfather taught me how to do that, taking me to see sentence
passed in the audience room, week after week, year after year.
At first I wept for every man who was going to die, but each
one meant less than the last, and in the end their deaths were
only numbers."

We reined in under the trees by the roadside, to wait for the
others. The country lay still, a yellow desert in the blur of heat,
and the horses cropped slowly at the long grass, too hot to shake
away the black buzzing flies.

"I heard that you are to be married," I said sleepily, leaning
back and letting my arms hang limp down the sweat-streaked
flanks of my horse. "That must annoy your sister. Lodovico of
Bari is supposed to be as rich as King Charles of France."

Beatrice laughed. "Oh, I'm second best as usual. The Duke

wanted to marry Isabella, but since she was already betrothed to the Marquis of Mantua, he had to make do with me instead."

"Have you met him yet?"

"No, but I've heard all about him. He's rich, clever, handsome and a duke. That's all I need to know." She laughed at my doubting face.

"Isn't he rather old for you?"

"He's younger than my father."

"How can he be so rich? Doesn't his nephew, the Duke of Milan, own everything?"

"I promised to tell you about Gian, didn't I?" Beatrice was full of her superior knowledge. She leant across and spoke in a conspiratorial whisper, although there was nobody to hear except the trees and birds.

"The Duke of Milan is . . . peculiar."

"Mad?"

"Not exactly. I don't know quite how to explain it."

I don't think she knew herself.

"Anyway," she said quickly, before I could ask any more awkward questions, "he wanted his uncle to rule for him. Lodovico acts as the Duke in Milan, while the real Duke, Gian Galeazzo, lives in the country. Lodovico governs and decides how the money is to be used, so it really belongs to him, doesn't it?"

I was silenced by this curious logic.

We turned together as our companions came up. One of the ladies in waiting hurried forward, a scrawny woman whose bad temper came from having no natural protection from the bumps in the road. Her voice was shrill and angry.

"What *would* your mother think of you, my lady? Racing along the road as though you were a couple of post couriers! I suppose *she* encouraged you."

"Our horses were startled. Some birds flew in front of them."
Beatrice smiled kindly at her.

"What will I do at Ferrara?" I asked after the thin lady had
gone angrily away. "Shall I be like a lady in waiting?"

Beatrice held out her hand. "You will be the sister I should
have had."

The late afternoon light turned the distant towers into a
gilded Babylon.

"That's our castle, the four towers with flags on top." Beatrice
leaned forward to point. "Over there, where you can see the
river, that's Belriguardo, where we go boating and have dances
in the summer. The long red building nearest to us is Schifanoia.
That's the nicest of our homes. I think so, anyway."

I nodded, looking down at the soft red brick buildings that
rose from the marshy plain. I was suddenly frightened. It felt
as though I were being reborn, starting again in a city I did not
know, with a family I could hardly remember.

Beatrice saw my expression and patted my hand. "They'll all
love you, I promise."

The castle looked more like a prison than a home to me.
The shadows of its heavy towers darkened the cobbles on the
streets and, as we crossed the drawbridge, the swans in the
moat arched their necks up towards us and hissed.

I followed Beatrice away from the clatter and commotion
in the courtyard. Out of sight of the courtiers, she picked
up her skirts and ran up the marble staircases and passages,
legs and arms flying everywhere. She slid to a halt in front
of a door and put a finger to her lips, then opened the door
very quietly.

The Duchess Leonora was bent over her silk embroidery
in one of the window seats. She was very stout, comfortingly

so, but she ran towards us with surprising agility. Beatrice almost disappeared in her embrace. The Duchess held her at arms length and looked her up and down. She sighed.

"Oh dear. I had hoped that you would have lost that baby fat by now. Isabella's figure is so pretty, too."

"This is Caterina, Mamma," Beatrice said, extricating herself. The Duchess bore down on me like a bolster. I smiled and curtsied. She was so full of soft sympathy that I almost wept. "Poor child, I was so grieved to hear of it. Your dear mother and father, and that lovely castle. I suppose nothing was saved?"

Beatrice came to my rescue. "Where is my father?"

The Duchess was diverted. "He has been with Signor Zampante all this afternoon."

"Oh," Beatrice said, her small nose wrinkled in distaste. "Is that man still here?"

The Duchess frowned. "Signor Zampante is your godfather, Beatrice."

"I didn't ask him to be."

"You know very well that he made the request himself. I know his work is rather unpleasant, but somebody has to deal with the criminals in every city. I don't suppose he enjoys doing it, poor man."

"He's well paid for his work, isn't he?" Beatrice's voice was hard. I was startled by it. The Duchess, it appeared, was not. She shook her head.

"When will you learn that ladies do not talk about money, Beatrice? Your sister knew that without having to be told. Remember that one day you will be a duchess and in the public eye."

"Yes, Mamma," Beatrice said.

I could hear voices coming down the passage towards us.

"That will be they." The Duchess turned to listen, smoothing the creases from her skirts.

"I'll show Caterina her rooms." Beatrice backed away, but the doors opened as she spoke.

"Ercole, my dear, Beatrice has arrived."

The Duke paused. "Well, well," he said in a tone of complete indifference. Beatrice walked slowly towards him and sank into a deep curtsey. He bent stiffly and kissed her on the forehead. I looked on silently, remembering how Mario and I used to run into the courtyard at Maggiare to meet our father, how he used to lift me up to ride on his shoulders through the cloisters.

"And who is your friend?" The Duke's cold blue eyes frightened me and I looked to the Duchess for help. She laughed nervously.

"I must have forgotten to tell you. Surely you remember Caterina, Giuliano's daughter?"

He held a cold hand out to me, quickly withdrawn. "To what do we owe the pleasure of this visit, signorina, which to me, at least, is unexpected?"

I stammered and looked at the ground.

"She had nowhere else to go, poor child," the Duchess said in a low voice. "It will be good for Beatrice to have a companion of her own age."

"She has her sister," the Duke said abruptly. "Well, Caterina, you look like a sensible girl. Perhaps you will manage to make Beatrice as much of a credit to her parents as her sister is."

"Yes, my lord." I curtsied and he turned to his wife.

"How are the preparations for the dance going? Time is getting short."

"Very well, I believe. This is to be in your honour, Beatrice. It was all Isabella's idea."

"How kind of her." Beatrice did not look pleased. She kicked one foot against the other and looked up. "She knows I hate dancing."

"Beatrice!" the Duke said.

"I think you had better show Caterina to her rooms."

"Yes, Mamma."

"Now you see what it's like," Beatrice said as we walked side by side up the staircase. "Always Isabella, the paragon of virtue."

"You flatter me, sister." We looked up to where she stood, a smiling golden-haired angel. It was impossible to believe that there was only a year between them. I stared at the vision with my mouth open, envying the full breasts and narrow waist. Beside me, Beatrice tugged at her bodice and threw out her flat child's chest like a pouter pigeon.

"What *have* you done to your hair, Beatrice? It looks quite extraordinary." The vision moved down the steps to join us and smiled kindly at Beatrice, whose hands flew to her hair as she tried to hide it from her sister's sharp eyes.

"It's very fashionable in Naples," I said coldly.

Isabella laughed. "I doubt if that will be enough to protect her at the dance. We don't much care for *southern* fashions here." Her tone reduced my homeland to a nation of peasants and I felt my face grow hot with rage.

"I'll send you my own maid to try to patch up the disaster." Isabella patted Beatrice consolingly. "I must go and see if the musicians have arrived." She turned on the bottom step. Her eyes were narrow with malice. "We've heard no news from Milan about your wedding, Beatrice. There has been talk that the Duke of Bari may be looking elsewhere for his bride." Her gentle laughter floated back to mock us as she walked gracefully away down the passage.

"Poor Beatrice."

She shrugged. "I'm used to it. She hasn't changed. When it gets very bad, I think of what I shall do when I am a duchess. I expect they'll all be very fond of me then."

The dance took place the following evening in the beautiful, painted rooms of the Schifanoia palace. Since nobody asked me to dance, I sat in an alcove with Beatrice and her younger brother, Alfonso, drinking sweet Lombard wine and munching marchpane cakes. We watched Isabella, the centre of admiration, smiling and laughing, surrounded by the most handsome of the courtiers. She turned to look at us and her clear voice carried over the court chatter.

"One of you must go and take pity on poor Beatrice. Not one of you has asked her to dance. I insist."

There was a burst of laughter as they clustered around their goddess, and a groan, quickly stifled.

"Look, they're drawing straws for the honour of my company." Beatrice laughed brightly. "Here comes the loser."

One of the young men, indistinguishable from the others, came slowly towards us, his mouth in a set smile, his feet dragging.

"May I have the honour of partnering you for the next dance, Princess?"

Beatrice looked at him steadily. "I prefer to watch, thank you, Signor Marinotti."

He hesitated. Behind him Isabella and her little court were watching, laughing behind their hands.

"Go on." Alfonso gave Beatrice a friendly push. "Where's that famous courage of yours?"

Reluctantly, Beatrice stood up and held out her hand to the young man. We watched her moving through the fast, difficult steps. Now, with her face flushed and happy, she was beautiful.

"She dances very well," I whispered to Alfonso. He nodded.

"Isabella wasn't expecting that. She wanted to make a laughingstock of Beatrice." I followed his eyes to where Beatrice's sister stood. Her smile had faded and she had forgotten her suitors. As the dance ended, she glided forward from the crowd to join Beatrice. We saw her lean gracefully against Marinotti, turning Beatrice into an unwanted third party. They laughed as Isabella bent to kiss her sister's cheek.

Beatrice came back to us alone.

The atmosphere in Ferrara was very different to the sullen apathy of Naples. There was a freedom that was new to me. After our lessons, Beatrice and I used to take two pages with us and go riding in the still heat of the summer afternoons. On the hillsides surrounding the city, women moved among the mulberry trees, their arms stretched up to the branches, their soft voices like the hum of insects rising and falling in the wind. In the villages, smiling mothers brought their babies out to blink at the sun as we passed by; sometimes one of them would come up to offer us a glass of wine, a piece of coarse rye bread and shelter from the heat. There were always a hundred questions to be answered about the Duchess Leonora, who was loved for her sweet and mild nature. Duke Ercole was never mentioned. Beatrice said that he taxed the people too hard for love.

Sometimes we rode up to a hilltop where the air was thin and clear and the plain stretched like undulating silk below us. Above the twisting river, grey castles dotted the hills, gentle curls of smoke rising above them. We watched the tiny files of brilliant colours emerging from the gates to wind their way sedately down to the plain towards Ferrara. All the traffic of the north was ours for the watching. Bands of stiffly armoured soldiers galloped past, their horses sweating and snorting fretfully in the heat. A group of tired friars, stifled in their thick brown habits, toiled up one of the dusty paths. Down by the line of grey poplars, we saw the trading boats slide past, their sails half-blown in the gentle wind. Sometimes a sailor saw us and waved a greeting, but we were too far away to hear his words.

In the town, too, there was a life and gaiety that I had not known before. There were the days of celebration, St. George's races and the anniversary of Duke Ercole's rule, when we sat on balconies draped in golden cloth to watch the jousts and pageants. The plays were always affairs of diplomacy, showing Ercole surrounded by figures who represented the truth, majesty and glory with which it pleased him to think he ruled Ferrara.

Afterwards, there were feasts in the castle, the long trestle tables weighed down with great dishes of spit-roasted song-birds, whole sturgeons hidden under garlands of flowers and haunches of venison big enough to feed an army. But always Isabella's face mocked her sister across the table, and Beatrice and I remained the watchers of the court where Isabella knew herself to be queen.

One summer passed into others. Beatrice was now fourteen, and still there was no news from Milan of her marriage to Lodovico of Bari. The Duke and Duchess were anxious and irritable. Beatrice avoided the subject. Isabella smiled and referred to it frequently. For she was to be married herself at the end of the year. Preparations for her departure began in the autumn and the Duke's face grew long and gloomy at the expense of it all.

Isabella made the most of the occasion, tearfully asking us all for small gifts to remind her of us. She was not modest in her demands; emerald necklaces, rubies and her mother's favourite cameos. I hid the few possessions I had for fear of Isabella's sudden affection. Beatrice was bolder and asked her sister to make her a present in exchange for a pretty studded belt, but Isabella only gave her slow, catlike smile and said: "Dear sister, do you not remember what Valla said? 'Is there any greater extravagance than to strip oneself of one's own possessions and then to ask for other people's?' I shall keep my few possessions and my poverty."

"Cow," Beatrice said to Isabella's departing back. "When I am a duchess . . ."

"This year, next year, sometime, never," I said in a stupid chant and laughed.

"Why do you say that, Catya?" Beatrice said. "Do you think it's true? Everybody else does. They think I don't know what they say behind my back."

I didn't look at her. I thought she would be crying. When I raised my head, she was watching me, quite coolly, as if she was assessing my value. I found it unnerving.

A week later, we stood in a room above the courtyard to watch Isabella's husband arriving. Isabella pressed against the window, crushing her skirts, then started back as though a snowflake had bitten her breast, like a viper.

"Father, you said he was good-looking, and everything that I could wish for, and I believed you. How can you do this to me?"

"So he is, so he is," Ercole said, looking to Leonora for support.

"Mother, save me, your own Isabella," Isabella said, sinking to her knees in the most graceful and Leda-like pose. Unfortunately Beatrice laughed, bringing Leda to her feet, more like an outraged Valkyrie now.

"You can laugh, little sister, but although he may be ugly, at least he isn't putting off the marriage because he has a mistress who's prettier and wittier than his betrothed."

Beatrice looked at her parents. "It's not true," she said. "My Duke Lodovico can't be like that."

Fortunately there was no time for an answer. Gianfrancesco, the Marquis of Mantua, was announced. I was furious with Isabella, but it was hard not to pity her as she walked slowly forward to meet her groom. She was at least three inches taller than he. His ugliness was in some ways the most effective foil she could have chosen for her beauty. Gianfrancesco affected the new fashion of wearing a beard and this gave his square face the shape of a heraldic shield with two embossed points for his eyes. When he spoke, which was not more than was absolutely necessary, he had a curious habit of swivelling his eyes as though an enemy were about to attack. In fact, Ercole's description of a dashing *condottiere* lord did not tally with the truth. I thought it a sad fate for such an admirer of beauty as Isabella.

After her outburst she seemed determined to behave as well as possible, perhaps to shame her father into guilt. Ignoring the sidelong glances and raised eyebrows of her old lovers, her smiles, her blushes, all her movements were made an offering to Gianfrancesco. I saw her trying to talk to him at dinner, and if anybody could coax words from an ox, it was Isabella. The subjects she spoke of did not appear to interest the Marquis, who only ate stolidly and occasionally nodded. The only time he spoke with any animation was when Ercole leant across his daughter to ask about the Gonzaga racehorses. Gianfrancesco thrust his elbow along the table, excluding Isabella, and gave the Duke a lecture on these horses, which apparently were his own breed, trained to a degree of perfection that we all knew by heart by the end of dinner.

For the first time, I pitied Isabella, sitting back in her chair between the Marquis and her father, her face pale and expressionless while Beatrice watched her from across the table with eyes harder than agate.

The long winter seemed interminable. The Duke and Duchess felt the loss of their elder daughter, and showed it. The atmosphere was tense. Beatrice could do nothing right in her parents' eyes. Her marriage had been her talisman and now it was gone.

We had all grown to dread the visits of the tiny ambassador, Trotti, who brought us news of Milan — and tears and quarrels. The stories he told now were all of the young Duke of Milan, the odd one, who had left the ruling of his duchy to his uncle, Lodovico of Bari. Trotti said that he was impotent and that his new wife, Isabella of Aragon, had angered Lodovico by accusing him of casting spells to prevent her from bearing a child; she was also complaining of ill treatment to her grandfather, Ferrante, the butcher of my family. As the stories came to an end, the Duke and Duchess would look silently at the ambassador, waiting. As he shook his head their eyes would turn to Beatrice who stood in a corner, watching, saying nothing.

Too proud to show how much she cared, she had become silent and withdrawn, but at night I lay awake, listening as she cried herself to sleep in the next-door room.

Every afternoon she would disappear, nobody knew where. Nobody cared. The courtiers found her sad face discomfiting at their entertainments, and bewailed the loss of their loved Isabella.

I found her hiding place by accident when I decided to explore the north tower one afternoon. The small wooden stairs were dark and dusty and I had to feel my way up with my hands against the wall. At last I came out onto the flat roof of the tower, where the wind whistled through the battlements and the clouds seemed close enough to touch. Beatrice looked up from her book, startled, and drew back against the wall.

I sat down beside her out of the wind. "What are you reading?"

"*The Divine Comedy*," she said, smiling faintly. "I come up here every day, to read, and to forget."

"Poor Beatrice."

She pushed away my hand and shook her head. "It's the pity that I hate so much. Can't you understand, Catya? The way they all look at me and whisper behind their hands. Every time Trotti arrives, I come up here and pray it will be good news, that I shan't disappoint them, but it's no use. You don't know what it's like, knowing that I have failed them all, and not being able to do anything about it."

She burst out crying and I held her against me and stroked her hair.

"When I was in Naples," I said slowly, "my mother was once very ill and Mario and I went to see an old woman who lived in the valley and she made a magic."

"A *strega*?"

"If you or your brother know of one, I will go with you. It did cure my mother. She was able to leave her bed the very next day."

Beatrice looked doubtful. "The Church has spoken against them. My father would never forgive us if he knew."

"How should he know, if nobody tells him?" The more I thought of it, the more pleased I was with the idea. At least, it would give Beatrice some hope.

"We will do it, then," she said.

"The only one I've heard of lives in one of those ramshackle huts behind the cathedral. I heard Zampante saying that they plan to bring a case against her. Why do you want to know?" asked Alfonso.

Beatrice laughed, but she gave him no answer.

One night the following week, we crept from our rooms, hooded and veiled like two old ladies, and slipped out of a side gate before the startled guard could stop us. It was a dark, starless night, but the ragged points of the cathedral were just visible and served as our compass through the silent town.

Alfonso had warned us that the woman lived in a street that was notorious for its prostitutes and gang warfare. As we turned into it we saw a band of young men staggering along towards us, arm-in-arm, very drunk.

"What shall we do?" Beatrice looked at me. We shrank back into a narrow porch and hid behind the pillars, holding our breath. One of the young men lurched across the street and leaned against the other side of Beatrice's pillar. I was sure he could hear my heart beating. It sounded like thunder claps to me. There was a long groan and a sigh as he spilled his wine and dinner from his mouth by our feet. The smell was horrible.

We came out slowly as he disappeared into the night, then fled back at the sound of raised voices. Two of the men were quarrelling.

"She gave me a poem on the beauty of my eyes. Shall I read it to you?"

"She would not dare! By God, I'll tear your own eyes out if this is true."

"But the lady must choose for herself, my dear Guido. She was most . . . affectionate last night. I agree with you, she has a charming little body and her eagerness to please is so disarming."

There was a laugh, a gasp, a clash of steel. We peered out round the pillars. They were circling each other like sparring falcons, claws out, sure and swift on the wet cobbles. Now one of them lunged forward with a laugh and they began to fight in earnest. I shut my eyes as a sword flashed towards us and a body fell. We watched the survivor kneel beside it.

"Damn!" he said under his breath. He wiped the blood from his sword with the hem of his cloak and was gone, swallowed up by the creeping shadows.

I was shocked by Beatrice's calmness. She picked her way over the bloody stones without glancing at the body and looked back impatiently as I hesitated.

"Come on, Catya! There's nothing we can do."

I looked down at the dead boy's face. He had been very beautiful. I dropped my veil over the twisted head and quickly made a sign of the cross.

The witch's house was at the far end of the street. We looked up at the shuttered windows and peeling walls.

"Does she know we are coming?"

"Yes, one of Alfonso's friends . . ." Beatrice broke off as the door opened and a plump, round-faced woman looked out.

"We've come to see the Signora," Beatrice said.

"You're looking at her." The woman smiled at our expressions.

"Well, what did you expect? A toothless hag with a familiar at her heels? I have a sick husband and so I do this every now and then to bring in a little money."

We followed her in silence up the dark stairs into a small room, heavily curtained, dimly lit. The chairs were hard and uncomfortable and the room smelled strange, a mixture of incense and something else. I felt faint.

There was a knock on the wall. "Who's there?"

"Some clients, Giovanni. Go to sleep."

"Well, young ladies?" She looked at us. "What can I do for you? A potion, a love spell, something to give your skin the colour of moonlight, a curse for an enemy? It's all the same to me."

"Can you make a man want to marry me?" Beatrice asked at last.

The woman laughed loudly and leant forward, her hands on her knees.

"Another jilted maid? Ferrara seems to be full of them in the spring. What have you brought with you, a lock of his hair, a piece of his coat?"

We shook our heads.

"Well, can you describe him to me? Is he tall, young, stout, thin, lusty, cold . . . ?"

Beatrice and I looked at each other in dismay.

"I don't know, Signora. I have never seen him," Beatrice said.

The witch drew back and stared at us. "I warn you, it is not wise to play jokes here. I can make trouble for you if I am provoked, my dears."

"I speak the truth." Beatrice's voice was cold. "If you choose not to believe it, we will not waste your time."

The woman sighed. "I believe you, but you're giving me a hard task. Can you tell me his name, at least? I must have something to work on."

"The Duke of Bari."

The witch whistled sharply through her teeth. "*Now* I understand. Princess Beatrice herself, sitting in my humble home. I must tell my husband."

"No!" Beatrice said quickly. "We are here in secret. Nobody must know. Now, can you help me?"

"I can try. You have the money?"

I produced a purseful of silver and gave it to her. She tucked it briskly into her bodice.

We watched her as she went about her work, crushing bitter-smelling plants and shredding them into a tarnished bowl. She told us to look away for the last part of the operation but I watched through my fingers and saw her put the head of a dead rat and a tiny, withered finger into the mixture.

She glanced at me. "You will have to wait outside while I talk to the princess."

"Oh!" I said, disappointed.

The door was thick, and although I listened with all my might, I could only hear whispers and part of a muffled chant. It was over an hour before Beatrice joined me.

"Well? What happened?"

She stared at me as though she were in a trance. I shook her gently, but she only said in a whisper, "We should never have come here."

"But what did she say?"

"She told me of things in my nature," Beatrice said slowly. "Horrible things, Catya. I wish we had not seen her."

"But what about the Duke? She must have said something."

"Yes," Beatrice said flatly. "A messenger will come from Milan in the next three months."

He came on the fifteenth of August in the year 1490, a tall, elegantly dressed man in a scarlet cloak. We saw him from the tower as he rode up the winding road from the plain. Beatrice's lute slid from her lap to the floor as she jumped to her feet and ran ahead of me down the broad stairs. We reached him just as he was dismounting in the courtyard, brushing the dust off his clothes.

"Have you come from Lord Lodovico, signor?" I asked.

He laughed. "You are very curious, young ladies. You'll know my errand soon enough." We watched him saunter away across the courtyard and looked at each other in silence.

Beatrice was sent for an hour later, and I waited by the well in the courtyard for news. It seemed a long time before she returned. I heard her footsteps on the marble steps and ran to meet her.

"Well?"

"Look, have you ever seen anything so beautiful?" She pulled at a necklace of pearls hanging like a moonbeam round her neck and held out her hands. In the left palm, a flawless, square emerald, in the right palm, a violet ruby cut into the shape of a heart. She looked down and smiled with content.

"Isabella's husband never gave her presents like that." Beatrice was radiant. "I wish you had seen my parents, Catya! I have never received so many embraces and declarations of fond affection in my life. Imagine, my father kissed me — twice!"

"When is it to be?"

"In February. Lord Lodovico is sending a sculptor here to do my head in marble, too, and I am to have a whole new wardrobe!"

"How glad your parents must be," I said.

"Yes," Beatrice answered. "An alliance with Milan suits Ferrara well."

"I meant that they must be glad to see you so happy."

She stared at me and began to laugh.

"You are strange, sometimes. I almost think you mean it."

"I do."

"When my father said three months ago that he wished Isabella was marrying Lodovico, it was because he needed the alliance, and he thought he had lost it. I am the instrument of their happiness. Mine is immaterial to them. That is what daughters are for, Catya."

"How hard you sound!"

"And how naïve you are!"

We both laughed, but our eyes met and locked. A stillness grew out of the silence. I could not look away. Beatrice moved restlessly.

"What is it, Catya? Why are you looking at me like that?"

"I don't know. Perhaps I was trying to look into your soul."

"What did you see?" Beatrice asked with interest.

"I could not see it."

She laughed with light scorn. "What a ridiculous conversation this is. I still have not told you! You are to come with me to Milan. It is all agreed."

"You will have no need of me there," I said slowly. She kissed me on the cheek.

"Quiet, Catya! I will always need you. You are my sister and my friend."

I believe she still meant it, then.

"Is the court like ours?" Beatrice leant forward and Cristoforo Romano, the young sculptor, sighed.

"Please, princess, try to remain still for five more minutes. You are making my work very difficult."

"Can we see it yet?" She jumped off the stool and Romano pulled down the wet cloth swiftly.

"No!" He looked at Beatrice's drooping mouth and relented. "Perhaps at the end of this morning. if you promise to stay chained to your stool."

Beatrice sat down obediently and folded her hands in her lap.

"You were going to tell us about Milan, signor," I said.

"The people, its court, the city or its ruler? Specify!" He flourished a spatula and pointed it at me like a magician's wand.

"Is the court very different from this?"

"Grander. Noisier. Harder. It's very splendid, but of the two, I prefer this one. There is less artifice here."

"And tell us about Duke Lodovico's friends," Beatrice commanded from her wooden throne.

Cristoforo had a malicious talent for description and we laughed helplessly as he set the people of the court into motion, marching through the room under the lash of his tongue. Rosate, the stout court astrologer, led the procession, bowing and smiling to Beatrice as the new Duchess, assessing my position and degree of importance before giving me a brief nod. Close behind him came the poet, Bellincioni, declaiming his verses and strutting along like a little peacock in his new clothes. Then came Gian, the young Duke of Milan, Lodovico's nephew, rubbing his hand nervously across his mouth, his eyes never leaving his uncle, his hero and protector, while his wife, Isabella of Aragon, walked by his side with her head bent, to hide her tears, said Cristoforo.

Leonardo da Vinci, the Florentine painter, watchful, smiling, impassive, leant against a pillar of twisted stone, making notes of the expressions of the courtiers, if they were unpleasant enough. The procession was brought up by the Duke of Bari's seven-year-old daughter, Bianca, clinging to the arm of her husband, Sanseverino, Captain of the Guard and the most handsome man at the court.

Beatrice clapped her hands in delight.

"And what of the Duke of Bari? My husband?"

Cristoforo smiled at her eager face. "He is a remarkable man; intelligent, amusing, and ambitious . . ."

"But what does he *look* like?"

"Tall, dark, swarthy as a gypsy. They call him the Moor for that. His voice, low and soft, and . . ."

"Oh, I shall like him!"

He laughed. "Yes, all women like the Duke."

"Why, what do you mean by that, sir?" Beatrice turned quickly. Cristoforo raised his eyebrows at the sharpness in her voice, but he only patted the clay head.

"Come and look at yourself," he said. "The Duke will only look at you."

It snowed that winter, and the journey to Pavia for Beatrice's wedding was hard. Her father and her mother, Isabella and I went with Beatrice to keep her company. We said little on the way, for we were trying to keep out the cold, and saying a word was like dying a little. We were all waiting for the first sight of Beatrice's betrothed, the Duke of Bari.

There he stood on the river bank, dressed in gold and crimson, easily the darkest in the party. Beside him stood a man I recognised from the sculptor's description as Sanseverino, for a more handsome man I never saw. But beside him, half-hidden behind the Duke, stood a tall girl in blue silk that clung to her like the skin of a snake. I have never seen a face that came so near to perfection; fine-boned, small straight nose under a high forehead and a wide clear mouth. As we watched, she moved slightly and hid her face behind one hand, as though she were aware of our curious eyes. The Duke did not look at us, but turned to place an arm protectively round his mistress's shoulders, excluding the rest of the party. He bent over her coiled plaits and she smiled up at him.

"We seem to be rather unnecessary, don't we?" Beatrice said at my back, and her voice cracked as she laughed.

I looked back to see if any others had seen. In the next boat, the Duke and Duchess of Ferrara stared at the party on the bank with the fixed smiles that are considered good breeding. I knew that they had seen the movement as clearly as we and that we must take from them our cue of ignorance.

"Pretend you haven't seen it," I said to Beatrice quickly. "He won't even look at her after you arrive, I promise you."

She nodded. I saw the tears lengthening, pear-shaped, on her lower lashes. I felt superfluous. Everything I wanted to say seemed obvious, so I stood and said nothing. Even Isabella looked anxiously at her sister and tried to reassure her. But her words sounded as false to me as they must have done to Beatrice.

The Duke came forward to greet us, but he first turned with

a bow to Isabella. "You exceed all the ambassador's descriptions, my lady." Isabella curtsied and smiled sweetly. Ercole came to the rescue with a laugh too loud to sound natural. "Duke, may I introduce my *elder* daughter, the Marchioness of Mantua."

"Ah," Lodovico said, glancing past me with heavy-lidded eyes to where Beatrice stood stiff as a wooden doll. I wondered what comparisons were in his mind, but he turned to Beatrice with a smile, complimented her dress and gave her his arm. It was hard to hear him, his voice was so low. His mistress seemed to have vanished. We fell into line behind them as they walked forward into the slanting shadows of the bridge that crossed the river. I saw Beatrice's father and mother exchanging smiles and suddenly realised how much this meant to them. It must have seemed as though the impossible had come to pass, seeing their daughter on the brink of becoming one of the most powerful women in Italy. The roles of the two sisters were going to be reversed, and I wondered how Isabella would adjust to becoming Beatrice's social inferior for the first time in her life.

CHAPTER VI

OUR HORSES were held ready on the other side of the bridge, and with the sun falling slowly through the winter sky we rode up the Strada Nova into Pavia. I thought we would be flung to the ground as the crowds jostled and pushed up against us, fingering the silk covers of the saddles and staring at us open-mouthed. Isabella's pet dwarfs capered and mouthed among the horses, drawing their usual audience who peered and poked until one stout lady went too far and pinched a midget's arm. I saw her fall back with a sudden squawk, holding out her hand to her neighbours. "He bit me, the little devil." The dwarfs were left to posture in peace after that.

The ladies seemed to me far more beautiful than the Ferrara women, with their long loose hair and high, round breasts pressed out of their low-cut dresses. They were bolder, too, accosting the courtiers with easy familiarity and clinging to the embroidered reins.

In the background there was a constant roar of "Moro! Moro!" that rose and fell with the wind, sometimes reaching a deafening crescendo.

I forgot to stare decorously ahead and twisted from side to side in the saddle for fear of missing any of the great palaces of fretted marble that lined the route, their newly painted frescoes gleaming through the loggias.

"If this impresses you so much, you'll never survive the celebrations in Milan," murmured the gentleman riding beside me. I hadn't even noticed him before. Strange looking man. It wasn't a courtier's face, but I found it hard to define. He smiled at me through the lines that pain had cut in his face with its sword.

"Atticus Silvo, court classicist," he said and bowed over the horse's mane.

"Silvo isn't an Italian name, surely?"

"I'm no Italian, thank God," he said, and laughed at my shocked expression. "My family came from Corcyra, but I went to Constantinople when the Sultan was looking for Greek scholars. Then I came on a diplomatic mission to Italy, patching up a peace after Otranto, and met the Duke. So I stayed."

He pointed to an imposing building on our left. "That's where I've been working until now, the university, and if you look beyond it, you'll see the Duke's new pet project, the cathedral." I looked up to where a marble cupola arched against the purple clouds.

"Why do you thank God you're not an Italian?"

He shrugged. "Oh, they lack discipline and they mistake the arts of revival and imitation for creation. They also pursue pleasure with more determination than propriety," he added with a loose grin and he looked sideways at Isabella, riding beside the handsome Sanseverino. I wasn't sure if he was joking or not, and I did not answer him.

The crowds fell behind as we came up towards the castle. Lodovico had already dismounted in the courtyard and Beatrice was standing at his side, swathed like a child in her ermine cloak. In the snow the bright plumage of the courtiers made them seem like birds of paradise darting about.

"It's beautiful," I said, looking at the long colonnades that reminded me of Maggiare.

"The grandest palace in Europe," Atticus answered, too glibly. It struck me that he must be paraphrasing his master.

"Excuse me for leaving you." He swung easily from the saddle and I watched him walk over to talk to Beatrice and the Duke of Bari, a sleek raven in his long black gown beside the Duke's gold mantle.

As I watched them the Duke bent towards Beatrice and pointed at me. She nodded eagerly and ran across the courtyard to join me.

"Come quickly, Catya! The Duke is asking about you."

I managed to curtsey without shivering in the snow and kept my eyes demurely fixed on the Duke's shining, black boots. He raised me gently and kissed my hand.

"It is too cold for such formalities. Beatrice tells me you are her dearest friend. I welcome you as such. You will add to the beauty of our court."

Beatrice smiled at me. "Is he not the kindest man there ever was?"

The Duke laughed and looked at her affectionately. I thought I liked him well.

"We are going to see the state rooms, Catya," Beatrice said. "You will come, too?"

Sister Isabella was at her usual tricks, now that her husband was away. She clung gracefully to Lodovico's arm as we walked slowly through the rooms, praising his taste and his possessions in her soft, low voice. Beatrice admired everything, without discrimination. The Duke smiled at her, and listened to Isabella.

"Your sister should remain with us in Milan," he said.

Beatrice gave him a small, wan smile and said nothing. He turned to Isabella. "I have heard that your husband is to join us in Milan. A messenger came from Mantua yesterday."

"Oh," Isabella said. She frowned.

Atticus, who was walking beside me, whispered, "Just as well. She is a very dangerous lady to have for a sister."

I looked at him in surprise. "How did you guess?"

"I have two eyes. It doesn't strain them to see that."

Lodovico raised his hand. "This room commemorates the Visconti rule in Milan." Beatrice's father looked away from the painted smiles of the Viscontis and said to Lodovico, "A fine family, the Viscontis. An old family." The inference was unkind and embarrassing. We all knew that the Sforzas had only been established in Milan for fifty years against the centuries of Visconti power. Lodovico smiled.

"They were a little mad, you know," he said gently. "My Visconti grandfather, Filippo Maria, was hardly a normal man. I prefer to remember my paternal grandfather who ran away from the family farm in the Romagna to join Boldrino's mercenaries, and became one of the finest warriors Italy has ever known, God rest his soul."

I liked him for saying that, but Beatrice's father raised his eyebrows and did not reply. His family had ruled Ferrara since the twelfth century.

"Is this of you, my lord?" asked Beatrice, who was turning over the pages of a manuscript. We moved down the room to join her. "Here," she said. "And this must be your nephew?"

Her hand lay on a richly painted page that showed Lodovico raising his hands as though he were blessing the kneeling boy. Underneath it were the words: "While you live, my uncle, I live safe and happy." And the reply: "Be happy, my son; I will always be your protector."

The Duke looked at it in silence for a moment and sighed. "Poor nephew Gian, his only wish was that I should take the burden of ruling from him. His affection for me is very moving." We all turned at the sound of someone laughing. "A private joke," Atticus said, bowing to the Duke. I wondered why Lodovico had looked up with such a fearful expression.

Lodovico and Beatrice were married very quietly in the chapel in Pavia on the following afternoon. None of us was present. But when we left for the Castello in Milan the following morning, there was an end to quietness. Banquets followed each other in relentless procession until the mere effort of swallowing became dull. Each of the ten courses was heralded by one of the ponderous confections of Bellincioni, the court poet, who seemed to think that length could replace talent.

While he floundered on for the best part of a long hour, fighting for attention against the great dishes of stuffed peacocks that came in with fire spitting from their dead beaks, I watched the courtiers tearing the marchpane limbs from the cherubs designed by Leonardo. I looked at the artist, but his face told me nothing. I wondered what thoughts lay behind the practiced mask. He ate none of the food placed before him, and he seldom spoke. Only his eyes moved, flickering over the faces round the table.

The city bells rang day and night until I woke in a sweat, thinking they were in my head, and the crowds sang and danced after us in the streets as we rode wearily through Milan to another joust or play or dinner. Lodovico had spared no money to dazzle our eyes.

The crowning entertainment was a tournament that made the jousts at Ferrara look like peasant revels, and the gloomy faces of Duke Ercole and his consort showed that they were very conscious of it. Sanseverino won the applause of the day when he appeared leading twelve knights dressed in the skins of animals, their faces hidden behind Leonardo's masks of wolves and lions. There was a rustle of excitement as they strode towards the balcony where Beatrice and Lodovico sat. At a crash of cymbals, they flung away their costumes to show themselves in shining armour. I could not help thinking that Sanseverino had gone to considerable expense to show himself to the best advantage. Beatrice's eyes glowed like torches as he bowed before her to take his prize of a length of cloth of gold.

There were, naturally, many allusions to Il Moro's majesty, the most impressive being a swaggering band of knights in Moorish costumes of black and gold, a presentation that was most dutifully applauded. They had even tutored a genuine Moor, a giant of a man, to hymn the praises of the new Duchess of Bari.

I noticed that none of these theatrical compliments made mention of the true Duke and Duchess of Milan, although they sat at the front of the crowd in the seats of honour, but I saw the little Duke clapping his hands as heartily for his uncle as if it had been for himself. Bella, however, kept her hands folded in her lap and maintained an implacable silence.

Too tired to speak or move any more, I watched Beatrice in amazement as she laughed and danced away the days, seeming to grow in strength as we flagged and fell. The guests from Ferrara and Mantua returned home, but the gaieties did not end. Beatrice had acquired a taste for dancing and feasting now that she was the centre of attention, and where she led, the court must follow.

The first two months were the happiest.

All was well. Lodovico seemed to be as devoted to Beatrice as she was to him, almost too eager to please her. Her wishes and commands were obeyed without question. If she wanted twelve new dresses, a band of French musicians or a boar hunt, they were hers. The courtiers, most of whom were profiting from Beatrice's easy extravagance, praised her for the same skills she had once so envied in her sister. The citizens of Milan blamed the Duke for their heavy taxes, and reserved their love for the little Duchess.

One thing worried me. Beatrice had chosen Sanseverino for her close friend, her advisor on all matters, however trivial.

She was, I knew, flattered by his constant attention, his graceful phrases, the veiled allusions that promised more meaning than the words held. On the face of it, the friendship was harmless enough. Beatrice loved riding, Lodovico did not and his son-in-law was the best horseman in Milan. The Duke brought them together.

Sanseverino was the perfect courtier, soft and smiling, generous, tolerant and available, with a core of steel that did not allow for failure. I believed the court gossips who said that he had only married little Bianca because he wanted Lodovico's throne for himself. He had few friends, but nobody dared to cross his path. He was too powerful an enemy.

His only obvious rivals to power were the Duke and Duchess of Milan, whom Beatrice had persuaded to stay in Milan as her guests. Everybody knew that the invitation had angered Sanseverino, who saw each favour to them as a threat. Nobody knew exactly how he set about removing the obstacle, but he worked through Beatrice. I was present when he sowed the first seeds of discontent in her mind, and there was nothing I could do to prevent it.

We were hunting at Vigevano one warm day in early spring. We had been riding hard all morning, and the sun burned down through the thin layer of clouds. It was a relief to turn aside into the shade of the woods and rest. Beatrice pulled off her heavy necklace of gold and rubies, laid it carefully in her broad plumed hat at her side and lay back on the bank.

"Why do you put so much jewellery on for a hunting expedition?" I asked. "Nobody else does."

"She wants to impress the prey," Sanseverino said lazily. "One final burst of splendour to dazzle them before they die."

Beatrice threw a handful of grass at him and laughed with me at his anxiety for his blue velvet coat.

Cristoforo Romano was playing his lute, singing softly to himself while we lay like Beatrice, with our faces turned up to the sun. She sighed with content.

"I wish Lodovico were here."

"Perhaps he is — otherwise employed," Sanseverino murmured. "Some say that you are unwise to leave him alone so much."

"What are you saying, Sanseverino?" Beatrice looked at him. He closed his eyes.

"Only that Cecilia Gallerani is still at the court and that she, like you, is a very beautiful woman. Do you not remember? She was at Pavia to see you arrive."

"He never talks to her now," Beatrice said with confidence.

"In your presence. Lodovico is always most correct. He does not discourage you from these long outings, does he?" He paused, and leant over to stroke her rigid hand. "My dear, everybody knows why but you."

She was silent. He looked at her, his face full of a soft concern. "You must not worry about it. There is nothing you can do, yet. He will tire of her, soon enough."

Beatrice did not answer, but I watched her hand uncurling like a morning flower to lie in his palm. He looked down at it and spoke again with a fine show of hesitant delicacy. I listened, full of hate.

"You will forgive my speaking frankly, in your interests, Beatrice?"

"If you feel it is important . . ."

"Perhaps you would be wise to see less of your cousin Isabella, the Duchess of Milan." His voice was smooth. "Charity can go too far, and you have entertained them here for long enough."

She was not angry, as I had expected. "Lodovico told me to be kind to her."

"And she is your cousin," I added.

"I'm seldom conscious of it," Beatrice said brusquely, and turned back to Sanseverino. "For what reason, signor?"

"You will not be offended?"

"How could you ever anger me?"

"All I would say is this," Sanseverino said slowly. "Lodovico, as we know, does not always speak his mind. Your cousin Isabella is a slight — shall we say, embarrassment to him. He would not wish to see her as your friend. You see, before she came, Gian was quite content at Pavia, playing no part in politics. She is a very ambitious woman, unfortunately, and she wants to put the poor boy back on the throne. To be honest, there would be no place for any of us at your cousin Bella's court."

Beatrice sat back and looked at him, her lashes veiling her eyes.

"Bella, you must remember, has a son."

"Well?" Her voice was very low.

He shrugged. "You have not as yet. She is determined that her son shall become the ruling duke. She hates you, Beatrice. Remember that before you came, she was the only duchess here. Now, she is nothing. She sees you, wearing the jewels she considers to be hers, leading the dances, the queen of *her* court. Do you understand?"

Slowly, Beatrice took her necklace from his hands, bent her head to let him fasten the clasp of gold. "We must go back. Look, the sun is going down." She rose as she spoke and walked swiftly ahead of us through the trees.

"Can you make no better use of your influence over her than to spread spiteful gossip?" I said bitterly as he walked beside me, humming to himself.

"I thought it was time our little Duchess opened her pretty eyes," he said, smiling. "Is that such a crime?"

"It depends on your motives, signor."

He laughed and wheeled his horse away.

I put on my butterfly mask and looked at myself in the dark glass by my bed, and as I stared the reflection became a stranger whose smile mocked mine. I did not like her. There were dark shadows beneath her eyes and she looked more like twenty-five than sixteen. Four months of court life had left their mark on me. I thought of Maggiare and a sick pit of longing made me turn away and bury my head in my hands. I wished to God now that I had not come to Milan.

Yet nothing had changed outwardly since Sanseverino had told us about Cecilia and Bella. The two rival Duchesses were often together and Lodovico had talked with me about them, saying how glad he was to see their friendship. The court was more outspoken. I had heard people say that Beatrice mocked Bella behind her back and treated her cruelly when Lodovico was not present. I tried not to listen to the stories, but it was hard not to wonder. I would have asked Beatrice the truth, but she seemed to avoid my company now. I loved her as much as I always had, but she no longer needed me, nor wanted my advice. She knew that I hated the frivolity into which she had plunged herself and the whole court. I suffered for my honesty. Beatrice was closer now to little Bianca, Lodovico's daughter, who was married to Sanseverino. For Bianca loved dancing and acting and would talk of hats and dresses all day, if required.

As for Cecilia Gallerani, she remained at the court, but if Beatrice cared, she did not show it, much to the annoyance of the courtiers, who craved a scandal. They could find no fault at least in the relationship between the Duke and his wife. Lodovico still seemed devoted to Beatrice, but my first impression of him was wrong. He was a weak man and now Beatrice ruled him.

I sighed and pushed back my heavy hair. Perhaps I was being

overimaginative. I wished I knew. It was time to go down for
the evening's entertainment, and I slid my mask back into place.

The Room of the Doves was full of noise and laughter as the
courtiers tried to probe each other's disguises. Beatrice had designed them all herself and I bit back a laugh as I saw how she
had made use of the occasion. Each person had been given the
mask that best represented Beatrice's idea of his or her character.
I recognised Atticus in the black robe of a priest and joined him.

"It is an amusing idea, don't you think?" I said. "She made
all the costumes in one night."

"I admire her energy, but not her discretion. Power has made
the Duchess foolish," Atticus answered quietly. "Look again,
Caterina, and tell me what you think."

I followed his eyes round the room.

"I don't understand, Atticus? What is so foolish in a
masque?"

"Look at the costumes that have been given to Bella's friends
and allies. It is a curious coincidence that every one of them has
been given a disguise that represents treachery and that Bella
should have been made to wear a cardboard viper on her head.
True, the viper was in the Visconti coat of arms, but . . ."

"Green for envy of Beatrice," I said slowly. "She would not
be so cruel."

"And Cecilia's? You have noticed that?"

"I have not seen her yet," I said.

"She is here, well concealed. You see?"

I followed his eyes to the mask of a painted cardboard cuckoo,
which hid Cecilia. Beatrice's laughter rang out over the noise. I
saw her, by the fireplace, a peacock moth, fluttering around
Lodovico.

"Excuse me," I murmured hurriedly and walked over to where
they stood. I was both dismayed and curious.

Lodovico raised his hand in welcome. "What do you think of

Beatrice's talents as a designer? I think I shall have to dispense with Leonardo's services and employ my wife."

His amusement seemed genuine enough. Beatrice smiled gently.

"I am glad that my work pleases you," she said.

"My dear, everything you do pleases me," Lodovico answered and he put his arm round her, excluding me.

"I am leaving," Atticus said abruptly as I rejoined him. "I am afraid that I lost the taste for this kind of pageantry long ago."

He looked at me and touched the painted butterfly wings gently.

"When you have time to visit me, Caterina, I would be very glad to welcome you to my house, but I know how court life eats at time."

He brands me as one of them, I thought with a flush of humiliation. Aloud I said quickly, "I would like to come with you, now. I, too, am weary of the court."

It sounded too eager, and I was glad of the mask that hid my scarlet cheeks.

Atticus did not express any pleasure, but he nodded and led the way across the room.

"So soon?"

Beatrice barred the way, her eyes brighter than diamonds through her fronds and feathers. "The dancing will begin in half an hour and we are having a ballet choreographed by Leonardo afterwards."

"Alas." Atticus spread his long fingers in regret. "You must forgive me."

Beatrice tapped him on the shoulder and smiled. "Never!" She sounded just like her sister, then.

"Your efforts will be wasted there." Sanseverino looked down at us over Beatrice's bare shoulder. "He doesn't care for court life."

Atticus returned his cool stare and Beatrice, sensing the strained atmosphere too late, dropped her hand and turned to her escort. "I am trying to persuade Belgioioso to bring me back drawings from France of the new fashions there. Some of them end at the waist. Perhaps Cecilia might try them on, or off . . ."

Her voice faded and was swallowed up in the high pitch of court chatter.

I had never visited Atticus's house before. I liked it. Small, dark and lopsided, its low eaves bent forward in one of the twisting cobbled streets of the old city behind the Castello's high walls.

A fat, kindly looking woman, with a face like an old, wrinkled tomato, opened the door. She looked at me with obvious surprise and then at Atticus.

"Stop drawing conclusions from thin air," he said with a laugh. "Caterina is a very respectable young lady, a friend of the Duchess of Bari's. Now, cease wagging your old head like a donkey and find us some candles for the study."

I had never seen such chaos. Books and manuscripts were piled everywhere, stacked against the walls, on the chairs, even under the tables.

Atticus waved his hand around in apology. "Giulia never succeeds in restoring her idea of order to this room. She fears my wrath too much."

"Giulia is your wife?"

"By heaven, no! You met her just now. You must have a poor opinion of my taste! No, Giulia denies the fact that she is over seventy and past doing any work at all, but we are old friends and she is used to my ways."

"But you are married?" I persisted.

"I prefer not to talk of it," he said and I looked down at the ground in embarrassed silence, wishing I had not mentioned it.

When I looked up his face had closed as if he had drawn a veil across it.

"She died of the plague, two years ago," he said softly. "There was an outbreak of it here, a very bad one; half the city died. It is a terrible thing, Caterina, when somebody you love, as I loved her, lies screaming for death to come quickly, knowing nothing, seeing nothing, only pain for hour after hour. I nursed her through the last stages alone. The nurses and doctors who came at first were common criminals, out to rob the dead, so I sent them away. They would have buried her in one of the great city graves with a thousand others, so I took her myself in a handcart and made her a grave under the olive trees by the river."

"Why did you stay here after that? It must have been so hard to go on living in the same house."

"There are not many princes as tolerant as Lodovico towards my race," Atticus answered. I looked at him, puzzled.

"There are Greek teachers in Naples and Florence."

"I am afraid I misled you," he said. "True, I am half Greek. The other half is Jewish. Milan is almost the only place where we can be free of persecution. So . . ." He shrugged. "So Caterina is sad and disillusioned by court life and by her dear Beatrice. Am I right?"

I tried to explain.

"She never used to be like this. She never cared for parties and banquets and clothes. Her sister did, but not Beatrice. Now she talks of nothing else and we have nothing in common any longer. And I hate her friends. I can't understand it, Atticus."

"You mean you don't want to understand it," he said gently. "It's so much easier to understand people when they are the underdogs of society. Try to imagine what it is like for her, becoming one of the most influential women in Italy, admired and imitated in her every action. It's gone to her head. She's like a little girl dancing in front of a looking glass, showing off her new steps."

"Then you think she will go back to being the Beatrice I used to know?"

Atticus sucked the end of his quill thoughtfully. "No. I'm afraid I don't. Once lost, innocence never returns. I would blame the Duke's weakness for that, not Beatrice. He should have been firmer with her, but his pride at having married one of the Este family seems to have overruled his wisdom."

I looked at him in surprise. "Surely the Duke could have married whomever he wished?"

Atticus shook his head. "Remember that his grandfather, Muzio Attendolo, was a peasant farmer's son. Others do not forget. It might help you to understand if I tell you something about Lodovico's background. It is a curious story. Lodovico's father, Francesco, came here as a *condottiere* to fight for the Viscontis, and his victories, particularly against the Pope, made him indispensable. Visconti kept him here by promising him his only daughter, Bianca Maria. Since it was as good as a promise of succession and more than most of Francesco's colleagues could hope for, he stayed. There was a year or two of promises and postponements since Visconti was slippery and Francesco was shrewd, but the marriage took place."

"And did she love him?"

"Surprisingly, yes, she did, although they were poles apart. She refused all her other suitors and persuaded her father to keep his promise to Francesco. Am I boring you by explaining this?"

"Oh, no. I didn't know anything about it before. Please go on, Atticus."

"You were yawning," he said accusingly.

"No, my mouth was wide open with wonder."

Atticus looked at me suspiciously, but he went on. "Anyway,

Visconti died, and no heir was named, contrary to Francesco's hopes. He was forced to fight the Ambrosian Republic, which had taken over Milan, and, after a long siege, he won. He ruled here for sixteen years, with every honour except for the recognition of the Emperor. That is what our present regent also wants. And it is worse for him. For there is another Duke of Milan, his dead brother's son. And his enemies can always use that as a threat to replace him. You do understand?"

"Yes, I think so." I stifled another yawn, hoping Atticus would not notice. "But I'd much rather know about Lodovico and Cecilia. Why doesn't he send his old mistress away, if he loves Beatrice?"

Atticus laughed. "You are such a child, Caterina. Lodovico is very proud of being what he is. He models himself on the other princes in the country. A mistress is a symbol, rather like a sultan's harem. Cecilia also gives him power over Beatrice, you see?"

"How?" I asked crossly, still furious at being called a child when I was sixteen years old.

"While Cecilia is here, Beatrice cannot be quite certain where she stands. Lodovico is wise in that respect. If all wives had a permanent threat to their marital bliss, their husbands would fare much better. Mistresses have always kept wives in their places."

"Well, I shall have to be virtuous," I said, "as I am not a mistress — or a wife."

Atticus laughed and took me back to the Castello. I went through the dark streets with my head in a turmoil of confusion.

I had thought that the Duke was a hero and now it seemed that he was a villain. I went to bed in a reflective mood and my dreams were all of blood and executions.

CHAPTER VII

ATTICUS TOOK ME to visit Leonardo the following week. His studio was crowded with young men, standing round the artist at a table in the semidarkness. Atticus motioned me to join them.

"Now," Leonardo said softly, "if we take this candle and place it in the glass flask in a bowl of water, the refraction will cause the light to increase . . . so!" He stood back and the room was suddenly illuminated.

"Marvellous!" Atticus said. Leonardo turned to him with a smile. He waved his pupils away, but one hung back, a slim boy in a red velvet suit whom I had often seen walking with the artist.

"You, too, Giacomo," Leonardo said firmly, shutting the door in his face. "Can you understand anyone preferring the life of a sculptor to this?" he said, picking up a small, perfect lyre and drawing his fingers up the strings as though he were caressing a pet. I walked over to look at it. "Is it Florentine workmanship?"

"I made it when I was in Florence, yes, but you mistake my meaning. Imagine choosing to be covered in marble dust until one looked like a baker, sweating and no doubt stinking, when as an artist one can have a clean house and clothes, and surround oneself with music and all things necessary for a civilised life. Mad, quite mad!"

Atticus laughed. "What about the great horse, your one

concession to sculpture? I hear the Duke is frantic to have it finished."

"The Duke will have to wait," Leonardo said, coolly. "Princes have always waited on artists. You remember that I found the perfect model in Sanseverino's stables, a marvellous beast, but these hellish celebrations have been taking up all my time. Now our new Duchess seems to have the idea that I am an engineer of fripperies. She's always pestering me for ballet designs and," he mimicked Beatrice's voice, "one of your clever inventions, Signor Leonardo . . . Now she wants a heating system for her rooms. How is she getting on with the Duchess of Milan, by the way?" He turned to me.

"Oh, very well, I think," I said defensively. "Beatrice and she were pretending to have a boxing match yesterday, with both of the Dukes watching and laughing."

"Who won?"

"Beatrice did."

"Yes. Of course she did. She's a hard little wench."

He said it contemptuously and I flushed with anger, but he looked across me at Atticus. "And what news of the fair Cecilia?" Atticus shook his head slightly, and stopped when he saw me watching.

Leonardo sighed. "I almost could have loved her, so charming, and a delight to paint. I positively dread having to paint the Duchess of Bari, and I know she will make me do it." He glanced at me and smiled. "Must I try to be charitable in front of her friends? I suppose so."

"I wouldn't dismiss her so lightly," Atticus said quietly. "She's a far stronger character than the Duke, and if she can succeed in eliminating Bella and Cecilia, she will be an extremely powerful woman. I only hope that she will turn her power to good use and not continue with this wanton extravagance."

But Leonardo was not listening. He stood by the window, looking through the thin oiled silk at the square.

"Poor girl," he said softly. We joined him to look down at the hooded figure of Bella crossing the square and turning down a side street that I remembered leading to the Church of Santa Maria delle Grazie.

"Caterina?" Atticus turned to me with a smile. "Why do you not go down and accompany her? She is too much alone."

I did not want to be thought unkind, but I was loyal to Beatrice — and Maggiare was still too clear in my memory for me to wish to see Bella, except for the trivial meetings and commonplaces of the court. She talked of her father too much. I stood still, uncertain, but they were both looking at me expectantly. I nodded unwillingly.

"Bring her back here, if you wish," Leonardo said, smiling at my obvious unease, and he turned to talk to Atticus.

I would have liked to walk very slowly and pretend that I could not find Bella; but I saw them watching me through the window. It was a cold, rainy afternoon for summer, and I slid and stumbled as I ran after her down the slippery cobbles.

When I arrived, panting, at the church, she was already sitting in a dark corner, huddled in her cloak. I pushed past the schoolchildren chanting their Greek lesson to their tutor in the nave and went to sit beside her. She looked up at me with wide, frightened eyes and shrank away against the stone wall.

"What do you want with me?"

I gabbled nervously, my voice betraying my insincerity.

"I saw you in the street and I thought, not having talked to you for so long . . ."

"Your choice, not mine."

"How is your baby?" I asked, more from desperation than interest.

"Why trouble yourself with asking, Caterina?" she said

sadly. "You are too close to the Baris not to share their attitude."

"I don't understand you, Bella. Beatrice is always saying how fond she is of your son."

"She plays her part very well, better than I had thought if she has succeeded in convincing you." She hesitated and gave me a small, bitter smile as she saw me looking at her hands, clenched and white in her lap.

"I thought you knew," she said.

"Knew what?"

I watched her hands twisting and plaiting nervously in her lap as she began to talk in a small, tight voice.

"Do you suppose Lodovico is happy to think I have a son who has more claim to the duchy than himself? I doubt it. Before you came here when Gian and I were newly wed and there was no child, Lodovico used to mock Gian in front of me and the whole court, pretending to give him advice on how to make love to me. He would go on, quite deliberately, until Gian was too embarrassed to remain in the room. Do you imagine that the Duke was doing that for fun? He wanted to ensure Gian's impotence. I tell you, Caterina, he is obsessed with becoming Duke of Milan himself and nothing will stop him. I think he will try to kill Gian, and *she* will encourage him."

I could find nothing to say. Still she watched me.

"You really have no idea what it is like for me, do you, Caterina? You look like the rest of them with that little, superior smile for the ravings of a jealous woman. Shall I tell you?

"When we go hunting, she wears the jewels that should be mine, three times more magnificent than anything I possess. She makes sure that I am given a broken-down old hack to ride that keeps me at the back of the train like a common servant. When I come into a room, the conversation breaks off and I see her whispering behind her hand, smiling. She has taken away my friends and my position, she has flattered my poor, foolish husband into thinking that she is his dearest friend, and she has persuaded Lodovico that she is fond of me and that I am stubborn and ungracious. Oh, she is clever, Caterina, so clever that Gian would never believe me if I told him how she mocks him behind his back."

"If this is true, what can you do?"

She smiled then. "I have one card left to play. My father. He hates Lodovico and if I choose to complain, I think he would march on Milan with very little hesitation."

"Surely you would not go to such lengths as that? It could only do you harm."

"If I am pushed any further, I shall write to him," Bella said. "You can tell that to your dear friend Beatrice, when you report back to her with this conversation."

She drooped suddenly like a broken branch over the pew, and my anger turned to pity, mixed with shame. I stroked her long, black hair as she shook violently. Her throat was full of the dry, racking cough of tears, but her eyes were dry and tortured. The schoolchildren had crept up the aisle to look, their lessons over, and a circle of interested eyes met those of poor Bella as she stared round like a homeless spirit.

"Go away!" I hissed at them, but they were not going to miss the treat of a free spectacle. They drew closer, giggling and nudging each other.

"Will you go now, Caterina?" Bella said calmly. "I want to be alone."

I pushed my way through the horde of spectators, and walked slowly back to the Castello. I remember that I had left my cloak in the church and yet I never noticed the cold. I think my spirit was more chilled than my body.

There was a message in my room, summoning me to see the

Duchess of Bari. I went reluctantly. Bella's sad, sallow face was too clear in my mind.

I had expected to find her alone, but Sanseverino was sitting at her feet on the great gold and sardonyx bed, reading Dante to her. Beatrice raised her head from the cushions and smiled at me, languidly. She held a finger to her mouth for silence. I stood in the doorway, embarrassed at intruding on such an intimate scene. Beatrice sat up with a sigh and a rustle of silk as Sanseverino came to the end of the passage.

"Nobody can read so exquisitely as my dear Sanseverino." She pressed his hand. "You will come back later? We must plan another . . . *hunt* at Cusago."

There was no mistaking the eagerness in her voice. I looked at my feet.

"If it is your wish, it will be my pleasure," Sanseverino said, bending to kiss her plump little beringed fingers. "But next time, you will let me kill the boar."

"Ask Bianca to show you the bracelets I gave her from the Treasure House," Beatrice said. "I think you will approve of my choice."

He smiled without answering and glanced at me. "I believe your friend is shocked to find me in your bedchamber. Perhaps she has heard the terrible tale of the Duke of Bari's grandfather."

"What tale?" Beatrice raised her head.

"Why, that of his execution of his first wife, another Beatrice. She had a favourite page who came to her room to sing her to sleep one night and the reports that the Duke received of the occasion were . . . somewhat exaggerated."

Beatrice smiled at him. "*Should* my husband be contemplating a murder, I very much doubt if *I* will be the victim." They both laughed. I smiled, without understanding.

"You don't like him, do you, Catya?" she said, after he had
left the room.

"No. I think he is hard and shallow and making use of you
to do well for himself."

"How tactful you are, Catya, dear. Perhaps you forget that
he and his wife are my dearest friends."

"She's only a child," I said. I must have sounded jealous,
for Beatrice said, "Bianca may be eight, but she is Lodovico's
daughter and . . ." She laughed. "She's too young to sleep
with Sanseverino, isn't she?"

Beatrice picked up a small enamel box and turned it to and
fro in her hands. "You would be foolish to try to turn me
against them. I might become irritated, Catya."

"You asked me what I thought."

Beatrice's voice had changed when she spoke again. It was
soft and wheedling and I did not trust it.

"Catya, what has happened to you? We were such friends
once, and now you are changed. Always this long face and disapproving stare. Is it the work of that scholar whom you are
always with, or poor Bella? I thought you said you hated her
for being Alfonso's daughter, but you were with her this afternoon at Santa Maria."

She laughed at my startled face. "I hear most things, you
see. But, answer me, Catya. Why this change?"

"It is you who have changed, Beatrice," I said slowly. "All
these parties and banquets and clothes and court conversation
that I hate, they are your happiness. Now you have everything
you want, you no longer need me."

"And you feel cheated, disillusioned? Poor Catya, all those
dreams and fantasies." She bent over the little box and shook
her long hair forward to hide her face. "I am no different, but
I have learnt to hide my thoughts, as you have not. I can be
quite hard when I have to be."

She turned to look at me. "Above all, I am determined to do what is best for Lodovico and for the duchy. *He* should be Duke of Milan, for the good of the people."

"And for the good of Beatrice?"

She smiled, blandly. "Perhaps."

I stood up. "It is you who are living in a world of fantasy, not I. Gian is young and strong. I expect he will outlive us all. I can see no hope of your dream coming true unless you think of murder."

"You are wrong," she answered. "He is sick. The doctors have told me that. I doubt if Gian will live so long as you think. Anyway, that is what I wanted to ask you about."

"Murder?" I stared at her in fright, my hand against my mouth. "Beatrice, I was only joking . . . I meant nothing by it . . . you must know . . ."

"No, no," she interrupted me. "I was going to ask you to go to Pavia to stay with the Duke and Duchess of Milan. I have told Bella to expect you there shortly after they leave here," she said as I opened my mouth to object. "All I want you to do is to write to me, telling me all that she says. I know how you excel in interpreting motives and situations, Catya dear."

"Act as your spy?" I said bitterly. Beatrice's smile was sweet, but implacable.

"You could call it that," she agreed. "It is, unfortunately, necessary. Bella is a threat to my . . . our power and I think she is a dangerous influence on poor Gian. Catya, you say you are my friend, and I ask you to do this in the name of our friendship."

"I suppose I am too much in your debt to have an alternative," I said wearily.

"Dear friend." Beatrice held out her hand and stroked my cheek. "I knew that I could trust in you. Now! Let us talk of other things."

I did not feel inclined to start the conversation, but Beatrice prattled on in bright inconsequence.

"Sanseverino and I spent hours before you came, planning a revenge for Trotti. Imagine, Catya, he had the impertinence to rebuke me the other day! I was so angry! I thought we might turn his fear of wolves to advantage and let a cageful loose in his house. That would teach him who may give orders here."

"I don't think that would be very kind," I said. "He would go mad with terror, poor soul."

"All the better. He deserves it. Sanseverino was most amused by the idea, but I see that you are not."

She yawned, raising her hand and stretching in an exaggeration of boredom.

"Why did Trotti reproach you, Beatrice?"

She pouted like a cross child. "Nothing important. It was only that I told him I didn't give a fig whether Lodovico continued to see Cecilia Gallerani. After all, there's nothing like guilt for making a man reasonable. Isabella always used to tell me that. If I wanted to get rid of Cecilia, I could do it just like that."

She snapped her fingers.

"Then why don't you?"

"I am waiting for the right moment," Beatrice said airily. We both knew she was lying to save her face.

"Don't you mind that he sleeps with another woman?" I asked gently.

Beatrice shrugged. "Of course, but I don't intend to show that I do. After all, who sleeps with his wife nowadays?"

"Do Sanseverino and you . . . do you?"

The resemblance to Isabella was unmistakable as Beatrice smiled. "Well, he can't wait for Bianca to grow up, can he? And why should I wait for Lodovico to be faithful?"

Before I could answer she put her finger to her lips.

"I know the Duke's footsteps. Stay, and you shall see how I rule him. You may learn from it for when you have a husband."

The Duke looked harassed. He bent over to kiss Beatrice, reclining now like a plump houri.

"I have been hearing of your hunt at Cusago," he began in a low anxious voice. Beatrice cut across him.

"I was entranced by it, my lord. I wondered . . . Sanseverino suggested that you might . . . give it to me?"

"Of course, of course." I never saw a house given away with so little thought, and she gave me a triumphant smile.

"But you must be more careful, Beatrice," Lodovico said.

"Why? I'm not pregnant, yet." Her voice had changed. It was light and brittle. Lodovico gave me an embarrassed smile.

"You are too hasty, Beatrice. I didn't mean that, but to run in and kill a wounded boar by yourself with no help, that is madness."

"Any *man* would have done the same."

"Of course, naturally." Lodovico floundered and I felt very sorry for him. They were right. He was no match for Beatrice now. He approached her cautiously, as a poor cleric might draw near to the Pope. "I have been talking with the Duchess of Milan, my dear. She asked me if we would reconsider raising her allowance and allowing her to come to Milan in winter. Pavia is very cold then, I know. She feels banished."

"No," Beatrice said, turning from the window at last. Her smile was soft and loose. "She takes advantage of your kindness. You must remember your position, my dear lord." She suddenly dropped to her knees in front of him while I watched in amazement. "Who is it that the people love?"

"Lodovico," said the Duke.

"And how may he best return that love?" She seemed to

have forgotten my presence, sliding her hands down the Duke's velvet doublet.

"By keeping the usurpers from his people's sight, by showing his subjects the glory of his house, by suppressing the voices of those who speak against him or his beloved wife, by . . ."

"Dear God," I said and fled. As I opened the door I nearly fell into the arms of Lodovico's servant, Da Corte, but he drew back quickly into the shadows and was gone before I could question him. Intrigue against intrigue. There was no end to it. Only to life.

Bella wrote to me, a polite constrained letter confirming that they would be glad to welcome me to Pavia for as long as I wished.

On the twenty-third of July, my birthday, I set off in one of the small, open carriages that only the Milanese court was rich enough to keep. It was a day's journey of easy travelling through the soft, green Lombard countryside. With the sky as clear and blue as a china bowl above me and the heavy hedges tumbling their flowers down over the road like a canopy, I was as happy as a bird released from its cage. Pitying Bella, I wanted to forget the past and I saw no reason why I should not turn my job to a better purpose and report good instead of evil to Beatrice.

The courtyard was deserted when I arrived. I wandered through the state rooms and found nobody, but I heard the sound of laughter through the open windows.

They were in the garden, under the trees. I watched them from the terrace as they sat, fretted with light, their broad, flat hats hiding their faces. Bella looked up and saw me, pointed and then waved, the thin gauze of her sleeve fluttering in the wind. I ran down the slope towards them.

"I almost wish you had not seen me. You looked like a painting, sitting here in the shadows and the sun."

Bella smiled and held out a bowl of peaches to me. "Sit, Catya. I believe you know us all. My husband, Gian, my mother-in-law, the Duchess of Savoy, and Signor Bellincioni."

"How is my uncle?" Gian plucked my sleeve, and stared anxiously into my face. "He has not been to see me for three months. Have I offended him?"

"Must we always talk of your uncle?" Bella exclaimed angrily. "He does little enough for us."

Gian put a hand on her shoulder. "Don't cross me, Bella. You will be sorry, not I."

She shrugged without answering and turned towards me. "I am afraid that you will find life here very dull, Catya." There was a biting edge to her voice. "We cannot afford to compete with the grandeur of the Baris."

"The vulgarity of the Baris, you mean." The old Duchess of Savoy shifted her large bulk to a more comfortable position and gave me a penetrating stare. I returned it steadily. "I gather that you are a friend of Beatrice's?" I could see that it was no commendation in her eyes.

"I came with her from Ferrara, yes," I answered cautiously.

"She's a trollop," the Duchess of Savoy said calmly and Bella smiled. Gian turned on his mother.

"You will not say such things in my presence. I must insist that you respect Beatrice as my uncle's wife."

She snorted with disgust. "You, Gian, are an innocent fool, or you would not be sitting here, but on your beloved uncle's throne. Come, everybody knows about her and Sanseverino, and Lodovico is as bad with his Cecilia. It brings a blush to my cheek to see how low Milan has fallen."

"But are you in a position to give judgments, Mother?" Gian said with a silky vindictiveness that surprised me. "Is your memory so short? I remember after my father's death that there was a certain gentleman . . ."

He had leant towards her as he spoke and now he plucked off her white cap and shouted in her ear.

"My mother, the whore, has pronounced!"

He sat back on his heels, laughing and muttering like a mad creature, then stood up unsteadily and pointed a wavering finger round the circle of uneasy faces.

"Mind-poisoners, slanderers! God! To be surrounded by such a flock of vultures! Long live the Duke of Bari, my only true friend!"

He raised his glass and drank the contents in one swallow before cantering away across the smooth grass on his long, gangling legs.

"Drunk, again," the Duchess of Savoy said mournfully. "Can you do nothing to stop him, Bella?"

"What can I do? I'm only his wife." Her voice was flat. "We must try to keep our opinions to ourselves, Mother. You know what will happen now. Another letter to Lodovico, reporting our every word."

"Followed by the arrival of another dog or horse from Milan for Gian to add to his collection. I know, I know." The old woman sighed. "Lodovico's too clever for us."

A stout nurse came waddling through the grass towards us, bearing a white bundle in her arms. Bella took it from her with a smile and rocked the baby to and fro in her arms.

"How pretty he is," I murmured awkwardly in the silence. "You must be very proud of him."

"And what if my cousin Beatrice has a son, Catya? Where will my poor baby be then?"

Nobody answered her. Bella gave the baby back to the nurse and stood up.

"I'll show you to your room."

"I am sorry that you were present at such a scene," she said as we walked up the slope. "Gian is being very difficult at the moment. It is so hard to convince him of his duty and his rights as Duke of Milan. I often wonder if he understands."

"Do you think it wise," I asked hesitantly, "pushing him into doing something that he doesn't want?"

"But I am only trying to support him," she said quickly. "Lodovico's place should be his, and as his wife, it is my duty to work to that end."

"But do you think he would be strong enough to rule? He seems so . . . wild, so volatile."

"He would have me to help him," Bella said simply. I shivered, remembering that she had learnt the art of ruling from her grandfather, Ferrante.

I felt depression closing in on me like a shroud as the days crept into months at Pavia. In Milan, at least, the tensions had lain beneath the surface. Now, my only happiness was in the letters that came from Atticus, telling me what was happening in the world where I already felt forgotten.

In Florence, Lorenzo had died, and his son Piero lacked the shrewd brilliance by which the Medici family had enthralled the city. Instead, Florence was turning from art to religion under the fanatical influence of Savonarola. In Naples, Ferrante and his son were in terror of the invasion planned by King Charles of France. Atticus said that Lodovico and Beatrice were siding with the French, although everyone in Italy knew that King Charles would look for more Italian conquests than Naples. Beatrice was at last pregnant, news that came as a blow to Bella's hopes for her son. La Gallerani, too, was expecting a child by Lodovico and the atmosphere at court was strained. Sanseverino, he said, was making trouble as usual, spreading reports that Bella had tried to poison Gian's servants, and Lodovico had written to complain to King Ferrante. Bella wept when I told her.

The little Duke often sought my company in preference to that of his mother and his wife, and I found myself growing very fond of him. His gentleness and anxiety to please aroused the same affection for him in me that he felt for his horses and greyhounds. Only when he was drunk or in one of his unpredictable moods did Gian become an impossible companion.

"Do you never feel lonely, living at Pavia?" I asked him one day. Gian stared at me in amazement, then burst out laughing.

"Lonely? With all my dogs and horses? They're better friends than my uncle's courtiers, Catya. They will never betray me."

"But don't you ever want to live in Milan? You are the Duke, after all, Gian."

"You sound like Bella," he said suspiciously. "I thought you said you understood me."

"I do; I only wondered."

"Why should I want to be Duke? Lodovico looks after me and conducts all the state affairs. Bella seems to think I am treated unjustly, but it was my choice, not my uncle's."

"Was it?"

"Oh, yes," Gian said eagerly. "That's what they never understand. I had to persuade him to rule for me, and he was very reluctant."

What could I say? A blind and deaf man could have seen through the Duke of Bari's reluctance to rule, and yet Gian stubbornly insisted that it was an act of kindness, not usurpation.

But Gian had a darker side, which I never mentioned in my carefully composed letters to Beatrice. Instead, I filled them with the stories I knew would please her; that Pavia was a dull court compared to Milan, that Bella's beauty had faded and that Gian was always praising Beatrice and saying how beautiful she was. I never said that night after night I was kept awake by the sound of screams and running footsteps. Nobody would tell me what they meant. Their faces closed against me when I asked.

One night, three months after my arrival, the sounds woke me at midnight. After two hours, curiosity overcame my fear. I slipped out of my room and felt my way down the unlit passage.

I hate the dark with its suffocating strength, the forces that I feel but cannot see. It took all my courage to walk on down the passage past the shining marble faces, frozen in the moonlight. No reclining nymphs and dryads here, but the harsh, brutal faces of Gian's Visconti forebears. I stopped once, but the screams rose to a crescendo and after a moment I hurried on with my head bent.

I stopped at the open door when I saw Bella twisting and cringing on the floor, her white robe patched with scarlet, her hair damp and clinging like weed to her pale face. Gian stood over her, pulling a thong of leather between his fingers. The screams I had heard were his excitement, not her fear. I could see his eyeballs, very large and white, almost without pupils. Too much of a coward to intervene, I fled back to my room, but Bella's tortured face was with me in the whispering darkness, and I could not sleep.

November. December. Bella was heavy with child. The leaves hung like battered rags on the trees in the park and rain dripped and trickled from the gutters and roofs. Day after day I sat, stifling boredom behind my hand, while Bella and the old Duchess talked in their soft, monotonous voices of dead years, coloured to a perfection they never had by nostalgia and discontent.

Etiquette demanded that Bella's child be born at their official residence in Milan, and I went with her from Pavia, with no desire ever to return.

CHAPTER VIII

JANUARY. One o'clock in the morning. The state rooms of
the Castello were hot, heavy with the smell of the crowds who
waited for the news. I was exhausted, having been there since
six in the evening. I lay back in a corner chair and watched.
Sanseverino and his friends were the noisiest group, arguing
over their bets on the baby. Sixty to forty it will be a girl.
Cecilia was leaning back against a wall, her face hidden behind
a veil of hair. She must have been able to hear the speculative
whispers passing from group to group. "Of course, *she'll* go if
it's a boy." "Oh, no question about it." "Mind you, she had a
long run. Too pleased with herself by half, if you ask me."
"All those intellectual airs. They won't help her now."

At two, the doors to the private apartments were opened and
I clutched the side of my chair. The excitement was infectious.
Rosate stood above us, letting the tension pull tight before he
released the announcement.

"The Duchess of Bari has given birth to a baby boy. Long live
the Duke!"

"Damn!"

Sanseverino threw a handful of coins onto the table. "Sixty
ducats nearer bankruptcy."

Silence fell as, one by one, they turned to stare at Cecilia. She
looked like a ghost, but her eyes were fixed unwaveringly on the
astrologer, Rosate. He saw her, gave an almost imperceptible
shrug of his shoulders and left the room. Lodovico had been

generous when her child was born, but now Beatrice could crack the whip.

The splendour of the celebrations made me understand Bella's fears for her own son's future. There had been little rejoicing at his birth. Now, the church bells rang in every village in Lombardy, debtors and criminals were all set free, money flowed into the people's pockets as fast as it ran out again and the singing and dancing went on from morning to night.

Bella had been brought to bed with a girl on the same day and after a week Rosate declared baby day for both Duchesses, as competitive in birth as they were in life. Naturally, the crowds were drawn to Beatrice. The more extravagant the spectacle, the bigger the audience.

I went to see her at the end of the day, when the visitors had gone. She was sitting up in bed, with the baby in her arms, laughing at Lodovico as he examined its minute features. My spirits lifted when I saw her. With her hair hanging loose and cheeks like peonies, she was the Beatrice I thought had gone forever.

The Duke came forward to greet me and kissed me on both cheeks.

"He is only trying to make me jealous," Beatrice said, smiling and holding up the baby. "Come and look at him, Catya. Isn't he a pretty baby?"

"Beautiful," I said, picking up one of his tiny, flaccid hands and spreading it on my palm like a starfish. The baby howled, most dismally. Beatrice snatched it back and rocked it energetically. The howls increased and the Duke smiled behind his hand.

"Get the nurse, Lodovico! I don't know how to stop it crying. There, there. Quiet!"

She did not look at ease in her maternal role. She was more used to quieting a frightened colt than a baby.

The nurse, a long, gloomy stringbean of a woman, glared at us accusingly as she took charge of the yelling bundle.

"You've been tiring him out, haven't you? Poor little creature!"

She whisked it out of sight round the door. Beatrice made a face at her retreating back. "I loathe that woman. She has no idea of her place."

Lodovico ignored her. "What do you think of the room, Caterina? I had it redecorated for Beatrice."

I thought the room was vulgar and ostentatious. "It's very unusual," I said.

"She doesn't like it," Beatrice said coolly. She mimicked my polite voice perfectly. *"Very unusual."*

They both looked at me.

"I passed Cecilia on the stairs," I said as the silence began to grow uncomfortable. "She seemed very unhappy."

"She has little reason to be," Beatrice said sharply. "We have arranged a splendid marriage for her, to Count Bergamini. It is a most illustrious family."

"The Bergaminis?" I had a vague memory of an old, extremely dull gentleman from some meeting long ago. "Don't they live on the borders? Poor Cecilia will never be able to come to court."

I realised my own naïveté as I spoke.

"No. That will be sad," Beatrice agreed, and her smile was like spring sunshine.

"You had something to ask Caterina," said the Duke. "Do you remember, my dear?"

"Oh! I had forgotten. Lodovico is letting me go to Venice when I am recovered, as his ambassadress to the Signory. My mother will come from Ferrara to meet me there. Will you come with me, Catya?"

"Oh, yes," I said eagerly, and my spirits lifted at the thought of escaping from the pomp and intrigue.

"Good," Beatrice said. "So. And how is poor Bella these days? You never speak of her."

Her voice was light, but her eyes were sharp and crystal hard. I knew her meaning, but I would not continue to play the spy.

"I haven't seen much of her since we returned from Pavia," I said. "And what I see, I pity."

"There!" she looked at Lodovico. "You heard that. Now what can there possibly be to pity about her?"

I looked at her despairingly. "She asks for so little, Beatrice. Can you not come to some agreement with her?"

"Not while her husband lives," Lodovico said, and stopped.

"What?"

"In such a way," Beatrice finished smoothly.

"Exactly," Lodovico said. "Well, I must leave you. Leonardo wants to see me about the money for his painting of the Virgin of the Rocks. He'll never finish it, anyway."

"You are too generous, my lord," Beatrice said.

Lodovico smiled wryly. "I doubt that Leonardo would agree with you. I'll have to put him off after all the money we have spent on your rooms, my dear."

He kissed her on the forehead and left the room. I looked at Beatrice, lying back on the pillows.

"I congratulate you," I said.

"He is a pretty baby," she smiled.

"You must be proud of yourself," I said slowly. "Cecilia gone, Bella pushed aside. It is most impressive."

"I don't understand you, Catya."

"Do you not?"

"Where are you going?"

"To see Bella, since nobody else has done so."

"Poor Bella. Please tell her that she is always in my thoughts and prayers."

I left in silence, to angry to answer her.

Bella's bedchamber was cold and damp. I shivered as I came in and pulled my cloak closer to my body. She raised herself on one arm and looked at me without speaking. Her baby was in another room.

"Well, and how . . ." I began brightly.

"If you are looking for more reports to take to the Baris, you had better leave me now. I have nothing to say."

"I don't tell tales," I said.

"Don't you?" she said, then suddenly put her head in her hands. "This treacherous court! Oh God! If I could only be in my beloved Naples again with my good grandfather. One day he'll come with an army and give me the Milan that is mine. He and my father know what is just."

Her words were ill-chosen. They called up the hatred I had tried to forget.

"Murder is their justice," I said bitterly. "You would do better to curse your family than to praise them."

She lay still, lily pale against the stone wall, watching me.

"They never harmed you, Catya. Why are you being so strange?"

I had not meant to tell her. "Did you never wonder how my parents died, or why I went with Beatrice to Ferrara?"

"You told me. They had the plague."

"I didn't want to tell you the truth. I'm not surprised that you were never told the facts. My parents, Bella, died of a plague of soldiers sent to murder us by your father. They were fortunate to die quickly. Those of my father's friends who were not killed outright were left to rot in the dungeons of the Castel dell'Ovo until last Christmas when your father ordered them to be hanged. And you expect me to care about your family! I'll stand and laugh when Naples is in French hands and your family learn what it is like to be in exile with nobody to turn to for comfort."

"I'm sorry," Bella said. "You should have told me before . . . I did not know anything of this."

She put her hand out towards me. I moved away. "Don't pity me," I said. "It's too late for that."

"We should pity each other," she said sadly. "We are both exiles here, but I came with greater expectations."

She turned restlessly on the bed under the thin cover while I tried to hide my irritation. I wished I had not thought of visiting her.

"I am a proud woman," she said slowly, "and so is my cousin. I suppose that is why I am so afraid. Pride will always break pride and it is I who will break before Beatrice."

I wondered again at the fluctuations of my mind when I was with Bella. A moment ago I had hated her, and now I felt only compassion. Perhaps it was my own guilt.

"Nobody can see the future," I said with false cheerfulness. "Perhaps you will be able to reconcile your differences."

She shook her head. "If the Duke had married a weaker woman . . . Against her it is impossible. I tell you, Caterina, neither she nor Lodovico will rest until Gian is dead and Lodovico is proclaimed Duke in his place. I am fighting a lost cause."

I smiled at her. "Bella, you are imagining things. Nobody wants to kill poor Gian. They always talk of him in the most affectionate way."

"I pray you are right," she said, but I saw in her face that she did not believe me.

"I will come and see you when we come back from Venice,"

I said. "If there is anything I can say to Beatrice that would help . . ."

"I think you have said too much to her already."

I left the room as quickly as I could, before my anger showed. Her sobs followed my feet down the stone passage.

I was sorry for Bella, but I was glad when she had gone back to Pavia with her baby and I could forget about her. She would always represent what I wanted to forget.

Of course, Beatrice left her bed long before Rosate had read the stars and had given his permission. She was eager to begin planning for the trip in May. The whole court was involved in her arrangements and Lodovico, who had tried at first to restrain his wife's mad extravagance, gave up in smiling despair. Leonardo was set to work on mechanical toys to be distributed as presents, while Calmeta, Beatrice's long-suffering secretary, sat in her rooms at all hours, ready to take notes for her speeches.

I was kept busy all day sewing and embroidering dresses and Beatrice sat with me, talking nineteen to the dozen, making drawings of elaborate sleeves and bodices that were torn up as soon as they were devised. She was very beautiful at that time, glowing with a feverish, infectious energy that over-ruled every complaint and argument. There was no extravagance she did not adopt, to show off her wealth and power. She was running through the money in the treasury of Milan at a frightening rate. I tried to warn her as she sat in front of her mirror one night, trying on jewels to dazzle the Venetians.

"You're ruining your husband," I said as I fastened a string of emeralds round her neck. "He can't pay for all this."

"Nonsense," she said. "Gian is paying. It's a *state* visit to Venice, isn't it? Well, Gian must pay for my state."

"That's horrible," I said. "He's paying for you to supersede Bella."

She pushed my hands away. "Why should it concern Gian what will happen after he is dead?"

"But there is no reason to suppose he will die, is there?"

"I told you once before, Gian is sick," Beatrice said quietly. "We all know that he cannot live much longer, poor boy."

"He does not seem ill to me," I said stubbornly.

Beatrice's eyes flamed and I took a hasty step back.

"You ignorant little peasant," she said slowly. "Southerner! You know nothing. How dare you contradict me? I must have been mad to bring you to Milan."

I turned away from her. "I — wish that you had not." I looked back, hesitated. "I will go away now if you feel like this."

She put her hands up to encircle my neck and pressed me against the bed. She leant forward until her hair touched my face and as I looked up into her green eyes I was afraid.

"In order that you may tell your tales at other courts, make trouble for us, Catya?" she said softly. "No, you will stay, and you will say what I say. You understand? Gian *is* sick; he is very sick. Remember that and we remain friends. Remember, too, that you are in my debt for what I did for you at Naples. I warn you, Catya, if I ever hear that you have spoken against me . . ." She dug her fingers into my throat so hard that I screamed from the pain. The door opened behind me, and Beatrice's hands vanished behind her back.

"Beatrice! Are you all right? I thought . . . I heard?"

Lodovico looked at my pale face as I leant back, struggling for breath, then at Beatrice who was calmly brushing her hair, smiling at him in the glass.

"We were playing," she said. The Duke's face relaxed and he bent over her, slid his hands down to cup her small breasts. I watched in the looking glass.

"What a little hoyden I have got myself for a wife! What a vixen! But a very pretty one, don't you think?"

He smiled at my reflection, and still unable to speak, I weakly nodded my head. The long fingers moved over her skin under the velvet bodice. Beatrice looked at me and motioned towards the door. I went back to my room and knotted the necklaces tightly round my throat to hide the marks.

The Duke came with us for the first part of the journey to Ferrara where the Duchess Leonora was to join us for our visit to Venice. It was an embarrassing and unhappy visit, with Beatrice and her mother trying to outdo each other in magnificence. So seriously did they take this petty battle that Beatrice sent a messenger home to bring her all the jewels of the Treasure House to adorn herself and her ladies. Every remark was spiked with venom; Duke Ercole even asked Lodovico if Gian had resigned the throne of his own free will. I was not the only member of our party to listen with interest to Lodovico's answer. He stammered, evading the point while Ercole leant back in his carved chair, smiling coldly. Beatrice was quick to cover the awkward pause with protestations of affection for her dearest Gian and Bella.

I was relieved when we left the castle and divided ways, Lodovico to Milan to wait for news from Charles of France, and we to Venice. I forgot my grievances in the excitement of our arrival as the great, painted bucentaurs nosed their way into the lagoon where the water coloured and sparkled as brilliantly as Beatrice's diamonds. I stood between her and Leonora on the wooden deck, and thought I was in heaven. The salt sea wind blew past us and clouds trailed through the sky behind us like a flight of butterflies. Across the lagoon lay the bride of the sea, her spires and curves half-hidden in the wreaths of morning mist.

Beatrice, anxious to miss nothing, ran from one side of the boat to the other, calling us to come and admire whatever her quick eyes had discovered. Her mother the Duchess smiled at her delight.

"She seems wonderfully happy," she said in a wistful voice. "I had feared that she would find it hard to cope with her new position, but I see my worry was unfounded."

Beatrice was chattering to one of the courtiers on the far side and her mother bent to whisper to me. "Isabella's husband told us that there have been some difficulties between them and the Duke and Duchess of Milan. He said that Bella wants to bring an army from Naples to get rid of Lodovico, while the Baris are looking for help in Venice and France. You must know something about it."

Her eyes were bright and inquisitive, her voice was too eager.

"I know nothing," I said shortly.

Beatrice rejoined us. "Come and look!" she said, pulling at our hands. "It is the most splendid sight!"

We followed her across and looked over to the Lido. The shore was hidden behind an army of galleys advancing towards us. It looked as though a garden had been planted on the water. Each of the boats was covered in a mass of exotic flowers, and even strange, twisted dwarf trees that Beatrice thought were Chinese.

These were heralded by a battalion of the most curious boats I ever saw. They were long and narrow with high prows rearing in front, carved like dragons and devils. Each craft was manned by a slender boy dressed in scarlet and gold, who guided it with a long golden oar, dipping it swiftly from one side to the other with a graceful sweep of his body. These boats moved with extraordinary speed and lightness, hardly seeming to touch the water at all.

"Which do you suppose is the Doge?" I asked.

Beatrice pointed. "Lodovico told me I should know him by his cap, something like a bishop's. Do you see him? He must be a very diplomatic gentleman to have organized that boat on the right. Look, Mamma. Manned by Milanese warriors with a Moorish leader to represent Lodovico's nickname of Moro."

"They must have a very fine opinion of him," I murmured, for the gigantic Moor was surrounded by the most elegant figures of allegory, representing Courage, Justice, Temperance and Wisdom.

"My work should be easy if they rate us so highly already," Beatrice said in a whisper as the Doge's golden galley drew alongside.

The Doge did seem most bent on being affable, and Beatrice, flattered and delighted at being done so much honour, was at her best. Compliments flew to and fro as fast as words could carry them. The Doge smiled and Beatrice beamed. He drew our attention to a part of the pageant he had himself designed, a race between four boats manned by crews of Amazonian ladies, their muscular white arms flashing and flexing as they raced towards us across the lagoon.

"Gracious me!" an old bishop from Como said beside us. "What an extraordinary thing! I am afraid I cannot approve."

"Then we will have to try to survive without your approval," Beatrice said sweetly. The bishop retired, looking most put out, and Beatrice leant forward to see better.

"You see which boat has won," the Doge said anxiously. "I thought it would please you. The crew is composed of a mother and her two daughters, to represent the Duchess Leonora and you and your sister . . . you understand?"

"What a charming idea." Beatrice rested her hand lightly on his arm. "I see that you are a diplomat as well as a prince."

And the little Doge smiled.

We were sated with spectacles by the time we reached the Duke of Ferrara's palace on the Grand Canal. Even Beatrice had begun to look a little weary, for the Doge was a most formidable guide. She had asked him to tell us something of the palaces and he had taken his task seriously. The boat was halted before every one in turn and we were treated to a full history of the family who lived there, often stretching back for two hundred years or more. As we had never heard of many of them and their lives all sounded much the same, it was not very interesting, but in the cause of future alliance, we all nodded and smiled at our host's painstaking jokes and anecdotes, to the best of our ability.

Beatrice sighed as we toiled up the long marble staircase, too tired to take in our surroundings.

"The thought of a week of this treatment, and the letters I shall have to write to Lodovico describing every detail." She stretched out her arms and yawned.

"It is a trial you must learn to bear in your position, my dear." Her mother sounded smug.

"Perhaps you would like to help me, Catya," Beatrice said hopefully.

I laughed. "Not I! You have Calmeta here to write your letters. I am going to enjoy myself in the streets and markets."

"I envy you," Beatrice said wistfully. "And all I have to look forward to is the dreary Doge at the banquet tonight."

The ceremonies of the Venetian nobility taxed even her energies. She was up at six every morning, writing to Milan of the parties, the clothes, the speeches made the day before. At eight o'clock the royal barge drew up at the steps to bear the

Duchess and her mother, both leaden-eyed with fatigue, away to
the Doge's palace by the Grand Canal.

I spent my days in exploring, and when it rained I wrote to
Atticus or drew sketches from one of the palace windows.
In the mornings I strolled through the Square of Saint Mark's,
watching the Venetian women shouting and jostling round the
stalls at the foot of the Campanile. They told me that the square
had once been the vegetable garden of a convent, but it was
hard to believe.

I liked to go to Mass in the Cathedral and stare at the golden
mosaics through my fingers while I pretended to pray. The
church was always full of sturdy, square-faced women and their
offspring, too young and wild to be kept in order. Nobody could
hear the soft drone of the bishop's voice for the shrieks and
scuffles as the children pinched and pulled at each other behind
their mothers' broad backs.

By that time, the sun had been up long enough to take the
chill from the narrow streets and I could pick my way past the
gutters, looking up at the women exchanging gossip from one
window to the next as they hung out their washing, squawking
and screaming like a gaggle of geese. The black, high-prowed
gondolas slid past me through the dark water and I stepped back
from the stink of their cargoes, a sea of jellied blood and smooth-
scaled silver fish.

The noise from the Rialto market was deafening. The coarse
linen canopies over the stalls stretched along the water's edge
on either side, spanned by the marble bridge, where the ladies
came masked with their lovers to look for trinkets in the
jewellers' shops. Since I had little money and no lover, I had
to content myself with the market place. It was like being caught
in the backwash of a retreating army. I was flung to and fro
as the wave of women turned from haggling over the vegetables
to scream at their children rolling cabbages down the cobbles

to send the unwary crashing to the ground. I was caught myself once and laid out flat on the stones, my fine new velvet dress all covered with filth and river slime. Beatrice shrieked with delight when she came home and found me, disconsolately rubbing at my skirt, which only looked worse after my efforts.

"I hope that you, at least, had a profitable day," I said sulkily.

"Very." She sank down on the embroidered cushions beside me. "I was given an escorted tour of the city. You would think they had never seen a duchess before if you had heard them all clapping and cheering. Lodovico would have been pleased for they kept pointing and saying, 'Look what fine jewels she has,' and 'How beautifully dressed she is.' I like the Venetians."

"I can understand why."

"Naturally, I like being admired."

"You are hardly starved of admiration nowadays."

"True, but how can one have a surfeit? I am never bored by it."

"I wish we were staying for another week," I said.

"Don't you yearn to see Atticus again?" Beatrice said slyly.

I bent to flick at the mud on my slippers. "Why should you think that?"

"Oh, no reason. I shall be glad to see Lodovico. Being good always makes me so bad tempered."

"And Sanseverino?"

"Caterina," Beatrice said in a warning tone, but she was in a good mood today and after a moment she began to smile.

"You must not think I do not love Lodovico. He is the best of husbands."

"Malleable?" I suggested.

She nodded, after a moment's hesitation. "He needs me more than I need him and that is a very pleasant sensation."

"Power?"

"Exactly. It is very . . . intoxicating."

"And addictive?"

She shrugged. "Certainly I would hate to lose it."

"What if you do?"

She laughed and leant back. "Death, of course. What else is there?"

Leonora had come in, fanning her red face with her hands. She glanced at us. "What rubbish are you talking of death? There is a messenger from Milan waiting downstairs."

Beatrice yawned. "More instructions. Nobody seems to realize that I am perfectly in control of the situation."

Leonora raised her eyebrows. "I will tell him to come up here."

The page in Il Moro's mulberry-coloured livery handed the sealed scroll to Beatrice, who held it up to the window to read it. She leaned back against the wall and I watched her face change as the paper fluttered down to lie at my feet.

"What is it, dear heart?" Leonora looked at her anxiously. Beatrice gave a small, mirthless laugh.

"Come here," she said to the page. "Go to the palace and tell the Council of the Signory that I must speak to them in private tomorrow morning."

The page looked startled, but orders were his livelihood and he bowed and left the room.

Leonora bent over her daughter. "Tell me what this is about," she said gently. Beatrice looked up at her with wide, cool eyes.

"To put it crudely," she said, "Lodovico and his wretched French alliance have landed us in it up to our necks. That, dear Mamma, was a message from him to say that the French King has at last decided to invade Naples but we are to head the enterprise. So my dear husband, like the coward he is, turns to me for help because he is too frightened to stand by his promises."

Leonora stiffened and stood up. "You must not speak of your husband like that. It is not proper in a woman."

Beatrice gave her a wry smile. "You forget, Mamma. Nowadays it is the wives who fight battles for their husbands. Chivalry, farewell!" She flicked her fingers lightly against her mother's arm.

Leonora gave her one look and walked out of the room, so she did not see Beatrice drop her head in her hands and crouch against the wall in silence.

"I am frightened," she said in a small, faint voice. "What if I fail? They may not grant me an audience. I cannot go back empty-handed."

Strange to see Beatrice afraid. I had forgotten that she was capable of fear.

"But of course they will see you," I said. "You are the Duchess of Bari."

"Today I almost wish I were Beatrice d'Este again," she said softly. "I do not feel strong enough for such a burden." She looked up at me. "We never expected Charles to follow up his talk of invasion. He seemed such a weakling."

"Why don't you refuse to head the enterprise? You would earn the respect of Italy, and Bella would become your most loyal friend if you prevented Naples from being invaded."

Beatrice turned away from me and went to stand by the window.

"You know so little of politics, my poor Catya," she said, and I flinched at the scorn in her voice.

"Listen. If we go against Charles he will allow his cousin and heir, Louis of Orleans, to lay claim to Milan," she said, holding up her hand. "That is one side of the coin. On the reverse side are the Neapolitans, who hate us because, in their view, we

have pushed aside Bella. So we must join the French and keep
Milan. For if we joined Naples against the French, we'd lose
Milan anyway. The French have the best army in Europe. So,
there is no choice. We follow France."

"How can you be so cold about it?" I asked, shocked. She
looked down at me.

"Wars, marriages, politics. They are all only games of re-
arrangement. The change is only in us. I can make the moves.
You are affected by them."

She knelt beside me, took my hand in hers. "You are always
complaining because we have drifted apart. There is your
answer. There is nothing I can do about it. I cannot let senti-
ment rule me now. You do understand?"

"I still think you are making a mistake to ally with the
French," I said. "How can you trust them? They are foreigners."

Beatrice looked at me in astonishment and started to laugh.

"What a little patriot it is. If the French took over Milan,
would you support them, Catya?"

"Of course not."

"Well, then you must accept what we are doing as a form
of patriotism. We are saving Milan, from your . . . foreigners."

I nodded although I did not find her explanation very reassuring. "You should not worry so much," she said. "I shall
go to the Signory tomorrow and then we will return home and
calm my poor, fearful husband."

She patted my hand and left me to sit in the unlit room,
brooding on the strange complexities of her nature.

I was not alone for long. The Duchess Leonora came back
and, seeing that her daughter had gone, shut the door behind
her with a conspiratorial smile. I waited, rather intrigued.

"I want to have a little talk with you," she said, settling on
a large cushion. "About Beatrice."

"Really?"

She shook her finger at me. "Don't pretend you have not noticed, Catya. You're a sharp girl."

"Am I?"

"Tell me," Leonora said, leaning close to me. "Is she happy with the Duke?"

"It would seem so."

"But she never talks of him. I find it very unnatural in a young girl."

"She is old for her years."

The Duchess gave me a long, speculative look. "You are very unforthcoming, Catya. I wonder why. Perhaps you are more ready to talk of Bella?"

"She is a very pleasant girl, a little sad . . ."

"Ah!" The Duchess pounced. "Sad. Now, why is she? Can you tell me that?"

I tried to retract. "I think she has a naturally gloomy cast of expression."

Leonora looked as formidable as either of her daughters at that moment. "I am not a stupid woman," she said coldly. "Nor am I used to being treated like one."

One look at that face of stone was enough. I still bore the bruises inflicted by Beatrice. I told her everything, rumour and truth. She did not seem so shocked or horrified as I had expected when I told her of Bella's fears for her husband's life. She waived my anxious explanations that these were not my personal beliefs and sat back, deep in thought. I watched her, half afraid.

"I did not know that Beatrice was so ruthless," she said at last, and her voice was respectful.

"But it probably has nothing to do with her."

"Rubbish! If this plot *is* in existence, it is Beatrice's doing. Lodovico had ten years of opportunity, but he never acted."

"You mean you approve of it?"

She shrugged. "Nobody approves of murder. What a foolish question. But a discreet removal is another matter altogether. Beatrice would make a fine Duchess of Milan."

"Let us hope she becomes that through natural causes, then," I said coldly.

Leonora had the grace to look uncomfortable.

"Very well put, my dear," she said hastily. "I promise you I shall say nothing to my daughter. You are quite safe."

I doubted it, but I smiled politely.

I looked down from my balcony at Beatrice as she left for her appointment with the Signory the following morning. As she glanced up and saw me, her face hardened and I knew that Leonora had betrayed me to her, as I had betrayed her to her mother. She looked at me for a long, still moment, and turned her face away.

I was put into one of the other boats on the journey home, on the Duchess of Bari's instructions. It was her method of showing her anger.

CHAPTER IX

WE JOINED LODOVICO and the court at Pavia, where they
were being entertained for the summer months by Gian and
Bella. They talked of politics and the French threat to Italy
while I sat with Atticus, wishing that he would be less brotherly
and more loverlike. One night, I followed him out of the castle
into the courtyard, where the four towers laid a cross of shadows
and the Duke's guards slept at their posts.

The heavy moon hung corn-coloured and soft over the park
where deer lay sleeping in the long, wet grass and trees spread
like black cobwebs over our heads. It was ghostly, the silence,
with only the hiss of grass parting underfoot.

"Beatrice has turned against you," Atticus said at last. "Why?"

I told him of Leonora and her betrayal. Atticus nodded.

"There *is* a plan to poison Gian."

I stood still. "Are you certain?"

"I think you should know since we are to be married. I want
you to understand the true nature of things, Catya, and I know
that I can trust you to be discreet."

"Married? Who said anything about marriage?"

"Oh," Atticus said. "I thought we had agreed, I mean, I
thought . . ."

"It's the first time I have ever seen you look put out." I
began to laugh. "How did you expect me to know when you
treat me as though I am your sister? I lack Rosate's astrological

powers. Politeness over two years is not much of an agreement to go on."

"If that is your only objection, it's easily remedied," he said, and he laid me down in the long grass and began to make love to me. I did not protest at all. It was much too enjoyable. When at last he rolled away to lie face down in the grass, I pulled up a root and lay back beside him slowly sucking up the bittersweet sap. "Poison, you said?"

Atticus groaned. "Oh, the single-mindedness of women. I see that I shall be more persecuted than Mnesilochus in the temple of ladies. Do you know the play?"

"I want to know about the poison; then you can tell me about the play."

"They may not have begun to administer it yet," Atticus said, looking up into the black sky from his grass frame. "I only wonder because Gian is 'ill' and Rosate is his doctor. While you were away in Venice, I was summoned to the Duke's apartments. Lodovico was with Rosate when I came in and did not hear me enter. I distinctly heard the astrologer say that toxin could be infiltrated into the blood stream through medicines, without suspicion. Then the Duke saw me standing at the door and spun some very unlikely tale of finding a more merciful death for prisoners. Rosate left the room as soon as he could, and the Duke began to question me about his own popularity in Milan, compared to that of his nephew. The theme was 'when' and not 'if' Lodovico should become Duke of Milan. I put it to him that the likelihood was that Gian would outlive him, and he looked at me very shrewdly and answered that the Duke was a sick boy."

"Well, I went away and thought about it. I could only conclude that Rosate had been told to poison Gian, since he has easy access to his person. All I could do was to warn the Duchess Bella, which was not a pleasant task."

"Beatrice is not involved, is she?" I kept my voice calm, but I could not stop my hands from trembling. Atticus put them gently between his and held them still.

"Catya, I shall never understand your loyalty to her. You are extraordinary. The child you loved has become a hard, danger- ous woman. She will stop at nothing to get what she wants. You have seen how she rules the Duke. He does not dare to do anything now without consulting her."

I pulled my hands away and bent over my knees in the grass until my face was hidden.

"When I was a child, Ferrante's soldiers came and murdered all of my family. I was taken prisoner. Beatrice saved me, took me to her home, treated me as her sister. Do you wonder that I am loyal to her, even if she has changed? Do you wonder that I cannot love Bella, whose family organized that murder?" My voice broke, and I shut my eyes against the scarlet pictures of my mind.

"Poor Catya." He touched me gently. "I will not talk of it again. You should have told me before."

I trembled as his hands began to caress me into stillness, and we made love again, a gentle cleaving of bodies, and this time I was his equal and we were one.

He turned to me as we walked back into the black shadow of the castle, my head against his shoulder.

"Try to forgive Bella. She suffers so much already and if Gian dies, she will need friends."

I looked at him, and sighed. "I will try," I said gloomily.

News came to Pavia the following morning that the Duchess Leonora had died. I was sad, remembering her kindness to me when Beatrice had first brought me to Ferrara. I could never have loved Leonora as I had loved my mother, but she had been good to me, treated me as her daughter, and she had never let me feel an outsider to the family circle as Duke Ercole had done. He had been a hard man then. He would be harder now that her restraining influence was gone.

I lit a tallow candle to her memory in the corner of my room before I went downstairs.

Sanseverino came swaggering past me down the passage, dressed for the tilts. I stopped him. "Have you seen Beatrice? I wanted to offer her my condolences. She must be very sad."

"Save your sympathy for a more worthy cause, my dear," he said. "Beatrice is in her rooms, designing a black velvet dress in the French fashion; most appropriate to the occasion, don't you think?"

"How can you be so callous?" I said, turning away from him.

"Hark at the little provincial!" He flicked a finger under my chin and walked on, laughing.

"Pay no attention to him," Atticus said from his seat in the window. "He mistakes mockery for wit, as usual. Well, you will be back in favour now that the cause for fear has been removed."

I perched beside him. "Is that a good thing?"

"Very, if you keep your ears open and tell me what you hear."

I looked round the curtain at the sound of footsteps, drew back quickly. "What shall we do? It's Rosate."

"Stop acting like the heroine of a bad melodrama, for one thing," Atticus said crushingly, but he patted my hand before he leant forward to bar the doctor's path.

"Well, my friend, and where are you going with that tray?"

"It is the medicine for the Duke of Milan," Rosate said stiffly. "As you know, the poor boy is sick."

"Is he so?" Atticus swooped suddenly and scooped the tray

from the doctor's plump fingers. He uncorked the bottle and sniffed at it, pulling a face. Rosate held out his hand.

"Give it back, Atticus, there's a good fellow."

"But I have better uses for it, doctor." He gave me a quick, puckish grin and before I realised what he was doing he had flung the contents out of the window.

"Good for the swans," he said with a seraphic smile and returned the empty flask to Rosate. I burst out laughing. I could not help it. Rosate drew himself up and gave Atticus a murderous stare.

"A rather pointless gesture," he said deliberately, and went on down the passage without waiting for an answer.

"I'll tell that to Bella to give her a little heart," Atticus said gaily. "At least it's a spoke in the wheel."

"Do you think it was poisoned?"

Atticus glanced down through the window. "Poor swans . . . And now off you go, Catya. Go and make your peace with Beatrice. Tell her the news."

"I can't. She won't want to see anybody now."

"Rubbish. Sanseverino is no fool. Public sorrow, private joy. Go and find out."

I went slowly to Beatrice's rooms down the black-draped passages, knocked timidly at the door.

"Come in."

I heard a rustling of quick movement. When I came in, Beatrice was lying on the bed, her hand held to her forehead. The floor was strewn with materials, including some lengths of figured black velvet.

"Catya," she said in a faint voice and held out her hand. She followed my eyes and sighed. "I must do my poor mother justice."

"But those don't look like mourning dresses," I said, bewildered, looking at the lengths of scarlet and yellow silk.

"The French may be coming," she murmured. "One must be prepared, even at such a sad time."

"I am to be married," I said, smiling. "To Atticus."

"What wonderful news! When did you decide?"

"Yesterday."

"And you love him?"

"I think so."

She frowned. "He is not very rich. We could have made a noble marriage for you, Catya."

"Like Count Bergamini? I would rather make my own choice and live simply."

"How very admirable." Beatrice yawned. "As always, you put me to shame, Catya. I sometimes think you do it on purpose. Well, when we go back to Milan you shall choose yourself a present from the Treasure House, anything that you like."

"You are very kind."

I turned to leave the room, hesitated. "Beatrice?"

"Yes?"

"There is no truth in these rumours, is there?"

"What rumours?"

I stammered under her sharp eyes.

"That . . . that Gian is being poisoned."

"But how dreadful! By whom?"

Scarlet-faced, I told her. She shuddered and turned away.

"I'm sorry," I said, and ran to kneel by the bed. "I did not mean to say anything about it."

She allowed me to clasp her limp hand. "You were right to tell me," she said slowly. "I knew nothing of it. Of course, there is no truth in the story. Rosate is our most loyal servant and he has always looked after poor Gian's health. You do not believe I would allow such a crime to take place, do you?"

Her face was open and trusting as she looked down at me. I shook my head and smiled at her. "No."

I reported this conversation to Atticus and waited for him to agree with me that there was no plot. He said nothing at the time, but when Beatrice and the court left Pavia a few days later to go back to Milan, Atticus insisted that we should remain at Pavia. They needed us, he said.

Two weeks dragged like an eternity and I could not persuade Atticus to change his mind and follow the others to the Castello at Milan.

It has always been a sadness to me that I should have such unhappy memories of Pavia. It was so beautiful, by far the most exquisite of all the Lombard palaces, its four square towers standing guard over the broad swath of the courtyard, the fluted pillars of the cloisters. If I wanted to imagine the Garden of Eden, it would look like the park at Pavia, with soft low-branched trees sweeping the grass tips, curving lakes on soft even slopes sinking down to where the Po slides and curves like a grey, sleeping snake under the whispering poplars, on its way into the crumbling silence of the sea.

And yet I could find no pleasure there. I was bored. There was nobody to talk to. Atticus was always busy consoling and reassuring Bella, and Gian was forbidden visitors by Rosate. I was left to converse with the deer in the park, and although their eyes were sympathetic, they could only look at me.

I made a habit of going down to stand in the rushes by the lake directly in front of the windows of Bella's rooms. I would remain there for hours, gazing mournfully at the far shore while my feet sank into the mud. It was a wasted effort. Nobody noticed, and I caught a chill.

The final straw was a letter from Beatrice, saying that she was perplexed and much offended by our absence. I took it at once to show to Atticus, delighted to be given a reason to leave.

He glanced through it quickly and returned it.

"Well, what are you going to do about it?" I demanded. "I

shall have to reply. Shall I tell her that we are waiting to discover if she is a murderess?"

I could hear my voice rising and I stopped as he looked coldly at me. I waited until his eyes left mine before I began my case.

"Could we not go back to Milan now, Atticus? No harm can come to Gian while his cousin, the French King, is here. We have no need to stay here."

"Then go," he said coldly, and turned away towards the casement.

"I cannot go alone. Please, Atticus." I tried to touch his arm, but he moved out of reach. "I feel so stifled here. I think I shall go mad if we stay for much longer. Take me back to Milan."

In the hard grey light, I could see the lines of fatigue on his face. I told myself that he needed to rest in his home, before my conscience could overcome my wishes. I took his hand, held it against my body, forcing myself to speak in a calm, sweet voice.

"Suppose that it is true, and Gian does die. What difference will it make if we are here? We cannot afford to antagonise the Baris. There is no use in looking to Bella or poor Gian for security. We must think of ourselves, Atticus."

"Please don't go on, Catya," he said in a cold, withdrawn voice. "It is no use. As I said, you are free to go when you wish, but I shall remain here."

Curiously, I admired him more then than when I saw his reaction to the letter that came from Lodovico a week later. It laid down a simple choice. If we chose to return, I would be welcome at the court, and Atticus's job was still open, and if we did not . . .

Carefully, Atticus folded the letter into four and smoothed

it flat. "You must go and tell the Duchess of Milan that we are leaving tomorrow," he said, without looking at me.

"And what of your principles?" I asked cruelly.

"The first principle I learned was self-preservation," said Atticus slowly. "It overrules all others."

"You are leaving me now?" Bella said incredulously when I told her the news of our departure.

I folded my hands and looked at her. "We will visit you soon, of course."

She raised her eyes and they were fathomless.

"With a French army?" she said.

"No. Soon."

"It is you who has decided this, Catya," she said.

"Both of us."

She shook her head. "No, Atticus is my friend."

Discomforted by her wide, staring eyes, I held out my hand, summoned up a smile. "We must leave. Our horses are ready."

She looked down at my hand, and turned away. "Go then," she said.

I looked back at Pavia as our carriage rolled over the cobbles onto the road for Milan. It looked already dead. The black lancet windows were barred, the flags hung limply against their posts on the four square towers and the warm red brick was greyer than stone in the half-light. I pulled down the blind and looked at Atticus, sitting sideways in the far corner, his head bent, hiding his expression.

"I love you," I said, reaching across to touch his arm. "You are tired. When you are home, I will ask Giulia to put you to bed. She will be glad to have you back in her care, won't she?"

His lips moved.

"What?" I knew how uneasy my smile was.

"I have been weak, Catya. We should not have left them."

He turned his head back to the corner. I took out my embroidery and stitched in silence until it was too dark to see, wondering all the time if I had been wrong in agreeing to marry him.

When I returned to Milan, Beatrice remembered that she had promised me a wedding present. She took me with her to the Treasure House. On the way, we passed the Duke, talking to Sanseverino.

Beatrice dropped him a half curtsey and glanced at the letter he was holding.

Lodovico put his arm round her. "What shall we do about it? You are my mentor in these matters."

"Ignore it," Beatrice said crisply. "It is of no consequence."

"What was in it?" I asked her when we were out of earshot.

"Ferrante of Naples, warning us not to bring the French into Italy. Well, we all know why *he* is so concerned."

"You don't seem very worried by it," I remarked. She shrugged.

"It will be to our benefit to have the French here. They will make us strong. If Italy has any sense, she will support the French — and us."

She turned the key in the Treasure House door as she spoke and we went softly in.

"It feels like a church," I whispered, looking at the soft, gleaming piles of rubies and emeralds, the crystal mountain of diamonds and splattered heaps of silver coins. Beatrice laughed and knelt by the jewels. "Then let us pray."

I smiled uncertainly and bent my head.

"No. Kneel," Beatrice commanded and raised her clasped hands. Her voice took on the droning warble of a bishop.

"Oh, Lord of Babylon, of pride and pleasure, fill this sanctuary with thy glory. Let it be rich in the splendours we offer to thee in thine image. Thine eyes are like rubies, thy body made of gold. Thou cometh to us clad in the splendour of the world. Let us partake of thy body and blood."

She raised a handful of rubies to her lips and let them trickle back onto the pile through her fingers. I was shocked. It was blasphemous, but I did not want to quarrel with her at that moment. It would have been most inopportune.

She made me sit on the floor while she pulled necklaces and bracelets out of the great coffers and held them up to the light.

"All that I have is yours," she said, and threw a pile into my lap where they lay like a dead weight.

I picked up a string of small, perfectly matched emeralds, held them against my skin and smiled with pleasure. Beatrice frowned and took them away.

"They don't do justice to your beauty," she said, and dropped them back into the chest.

I was offered everything, and given nothing. Beatrice's excuses were feeble. I soon saw that she only wanted an audience for her treasures. When my admiration began to flag, she became bored and wanted to leave. I was stupid to have thought that she would be generous with more than words, and yet I remembered the casual munificence she had shown to Bianca Sanseverino, the jewels she had showered on her.

Atticus and Leonardo only laughed when I went to them for sympathy.

"And is she going to grace your wedding with her presence?" Leonardo asked.

"She hasn't said so," I admitted. "But she is always very busy. She may not have time."

"She always has time to divert herself," Leonardo said dryly. "But then there will be no audience for her at your wedding. You will have to console yourself with the Duke instead."

"God preserve us from such a fate!" Atticus exclaimed. "If

he comes, it means that a simple ceremony will be turned into a grand nightmare."

Leonardo smiled at me. "Catya will enjoy it, at any rate. There! You can move. It is finished."

I went to look over his shoulder at the drawing and saw myself, but not myself, a smiling Madonna, shadowed and long-eyed.

"He has painted your soul on your face," Atticus said solemnly.

Leonardo held it out to me. "Your present. Perhaps it will console you for Beatrice's non-offering."

"I would rather have this than a hundred of her necklaces," I said slowly.

"You are wise, Catya," Atticus said, and he held his hand to my cheek. Leonardo sighed.

Our wedding was not the grand affair Atticus had dreaded, for Ferrante was dead and his son, Alfonso, was marching out against Milan with all the troops of Naples. He had decided to strike before the French did. Everybody of importance was in council at the Castello, and I was in terror that the soldiers of Naples would destroy my life a second time.

The church was almost empty. Leonardo came with his sloe-eyed love, Giacomo Salai, both of them dressed like princes, followed by Atticus's friend Merula, the Greek professor, and Giulia, very smart and uneasy in a new dress that seemed to be giving her more pain than pleasure. She wept so loudly during the service that Atticus kept looking round to see if she was ill, whereupon the bishop coughed and waited very pointedly.

I could hear Salai's stifled laughter as each new disaster broke over our heads. The choristers did not arrive until halfway through the service, having played truant to join everyone else in watching the troops assemble. This confused the bishop who lost his place and began the service all over again. Atticus and I, bewildered, gave all the wrong answers while our tiny congregation fidgeted and muttered on their knees. It was a dreadful afternoon, and it was all I could do to smile, let alone speak to Atticus when we walked slowly back to the little house behind the Castello.

Giulia waited on us at dinner, giggling like a girl at her well-worn jokes about marriage. I stared at my plate of over-spiced broth, while Atticus talked about the news of the unexpected invasion from Naples, and noticed nothing.

"You don't seem very interested," he said at last, putting down his knife. "Am I boring you?"

"I am tired of politics," I said flatly.

"Why did you not say so before?"

"And interrupt your monologue? Oh, surely not, for that would be a crime."

I knew I was being childish and unpleasant, but I could not control the rising tide of fury that drove my voice on up the scale into silly talk that I am embarrassed to remember. I will not write down everything I said.

Atticus turned at last to where Giulia stood, round-eyed and motionless behind his chair. "I think you had better go to bed," he said.

She ducked her head and went, but not before giving me a long, reproachful look. I met it with bland silence.

Later we lay side by side in the dark, avoiding any contact, like two stone effigies on a tomb, while the light poked through the windows to mock us. I licked away the tears as they rolled down my cheeks onto my lips, and tried to stop my body from shaking. I felt Atticus stir beside me. He reached out a hand and laid it very lightly on my breast. I thought about it, felt it warm my skin. I did not move. After a little while it went away, and I felt deserted.

In the early hours of the morning I rose and began to move quietly round the room.

"What are you doing, Caterina?"

"Looking for my clothes. I'm going away."

"Oh, God!" he said, turned over and went to sleep.

I could hear him breathing gently. It was too dark to find anything and I was tired. I sat in the window and watched the shadows of clouds crossing the street, and then I crept back into bed. It was very cold and I slid closer to his body, for warmth.

When I woke, I was lying in his arms with my face buried in his neck and my legs twined through his. I smiled and rubbed my face over his skin until it prickled. Then I went back to sleep.

Atticus went to the court the next day to hear what the news was. He returned late and exhausted.

"Well, what are they going to do?" I asked, sitting on the study floor at his feet. He reached down and began to undo the tight plaits so that my hair hung loose to my waist.

"The Duke has collapsed from the shock of an army from Naples knocking at his door," he said at last. "There is no longer any doubt about who rules Milan. We all noticed it today. She has instructed Sanseverino to leave for France immediately."

"He must be pleased," I said. "He has talked of nothing else for the last month. Who knows, perhaps he will stay there."

"I don't want to dash your hopes, but I rather think Signor Sanseverino finds Milan a more profitable place to be."

"And what is the reaction at the court to bringing in the French? Talk is one thing, *messieurs* in Milan another."

"I thought that you were tired of talking politics."

"That was yesterday," I said.

"I see." He laughed. "Most people are afraid. I am, myself. The Baris think they can control King Charles as though he were a puppet, and I think they are mistaken. To the other powers in Italy, it will seem like a betrayal and traitors are not easily forgiven. Merula tells me that Savonarola's sermons have taken a hold on the people and they are terrified of what the French will do."

I nodded. "I was buying vegetables in the Piazza del Castello this morning and I heard a monk preaching against the dangers of invasion. You know what the morning shoppers are like usually. They listen for five minutes and then they start gossiping with their neighbours and drift away. Today, they were completely quiet and nobody left before the end. I even saw people beginning to cross themselves and mutter prayers."

"You should be happy, Catya," he said. "Beatrice has the power you wanted for her, and the admiration, too."

He pulled me up from the floor until my head lay on his shoulder, and we talked no more of politics.

Three months passed and the troops of Naples plundered the Lombard borders, but Sanseverino had not come back with the French King. Anxiety and curiosity took me to the Castello. I found Beatrice in her rooms, dictating letters to Calmeta. She smiled and gestured me to a chair to wait.

I sat, listening, impressed by her efficiency. Calmeta was hard put to keep up with her quick speech.

When he had gone, she sank back in a chair by the window and let her head drop for a moment.

"You are tired," I said gently. "I will come back later."

"No. Look! I am revived!" She pushed back her heavy hair and stood up. "Catya, do you know what's happened? The Duke gave permission to Sanseverino to consummate his marriage before he left. Poor little Bianca. She goes about looking whiter than a sheet now."

"But she's only ten!"

"Exactly." Beatrice looked cruel. "It can't have been very stimulating."

"And how is the child-raper enjoying his stay at Lyons?"

"Too much. I am heartily tired of his accounts of the King's rose-scented bed and love of romantic literature."

Her fingers tapped restlessly on the side of the chair. "I put a good face on it to Lodovico, but we are all worried. King Charles shows no desire to leave."

"Why not?"

She sighed. "The usual reason. A woman. Apparently, there is a very powerful antiwar party at Lyons. They have got a young girl in their clutches whom the King has been pursuing, and she has been ordered to keep his interest, without giving in to him. So — the King lingers and Sanseverino fills his letters with accounts of his friendship with Charles, how the King has given him one of his favourite mistresses and so on. As though *that* were of any importance."

She broke off at the sound of footsteps. They stopped outside the door. Lodovico came in.

"We are saved, Beatrice. Look at this!"

"What is it? Not from France?"

She snatched the letter from him and read it eagerly.

"Oh, but this is magnificent!" she exclaimed. "To think that I believed Sanseverino had failed us!"

"But it says Charles is sending Orleans ahead of him with the French vanguard." The Duke was worried. "You know that Orleans wants Milan for himself."

Beatrice took his hands in hers. "You will meet him like a prince," she said firmly. "Frighten him. Make him see how ridiculous his thoughts of claiming Milan are. You can do it, my dear lord. You shall do it. I shall prepare Annona for the King, and fill it with our most beautiful ladies. That is what Charles will most appreciate. Catya, you will come?"

I nodded joyfully.

"We must call a council," Beatrice said. "We need more money for this."

"They won't like that. We are being accused of extravagance as it is."

"Let them complain. They will have to agree. We have saved Milan from Naples. Is not that enough?"

"Now is the time to act," Lodovico said in a low voice.

"Hush!" Beatrice said quickly.

The Duke looked nervously towards me.

"Yes. You can leave us now, Catya," Beatrice said.

I shut the door quietly behind me and looked down the passage. It was deserted. Only the painted eyes of the Greek statues watched me as I knelt and listened.

"It is the perfect opportunity," I heard him say excitedly. "We will be at our most powerful. There is no risk now. We only need to increase the medicine."

Silence. Whispers.

"He will suffer no pain?" I heard her ask.

"None. Rosate is an excellent doctor."

"You are certain?"

"Certain."

I straightened my back and went slowly down the passage. I wanted to go and meet the King and see all the fine French ladies. I did not want to go back to Pavia at any cost. If I repeated what I had heard, I knew too well what Atticus would say.

I told him that the French were coming. No more.

He left two months later to go with the Duke to meet Louis of Orleans at Alessandria.

CHAPTER X

ATTICUS BROUGHT BACK accounts of Alessandria that made me laugh until my sides ached, and my delight drove him on into more and more extravagant descriptions.

"If you had only seen them, Catya! I have never seen such a display of hypocrisy in my life! Masterly, absolutely masterly! There was Lodovico, who had done nothing but complain the whole way from Milan, bowing so . . ." He swept me a bow to dust the floor with his hair. ". . . and Orleans, thus."

An overambitious flourish swept one of the plates off the table.

"Atticus! Are you mad, or drunk or both?"

"Maddened by your beauty, inflamed with desire!" declaimed Atticus, striking an attitude.

"I see," I said, laughing. "And then what happened?"

"Then we retired to talk while all the inhabitants of Alessandria clapped and cheered at such a friendly encounter. It was better than being plundered. But they were well deceived! No sooner were we out of sight than Orleans demanded a loan of sixty thousand ducats! The Duke was furious, but what could he do?"

"Refuse?"

Atticus shook his head. "It was the price he had to pay for the retreat of the Naples army. Which, I may add, was faster than a boulder rolling down a hill. They must be back in Naples by now. Nobody wants to fight the French. You should see their artillery. One barrage, and the Castello would fall down."

There was a discreet tap at the door. We looked at each other, laughter gone.

"I'll go," Atticus said. "A strange time of night for visitors."

I heard the high, shrilling voice of Bellincioni and groaned, but instead of coming in, he went with Atticus into the next-door room, and they closed the door behind them.

The hours plodded heavily by while I watched the food congeal on the table. It was past midnight before Bellincioni left. Atticus looked very grave as he came into the room.

"It's bad news, I'm afraid," he said slowly. "They must have grown impatient. Bellincioni rode from Pavia tonight. Gian is dying."

I looked at him without speaking, feeling suddenly very sick. "Was it . . . ?"

He nodded. "Poison in his medicine. It's the only explanation. We should never have left. Bellincioni says that Gian is very weak already, but when he speaks, it is always to ask if his beloved uncle is coming to visit him soon. He even keeps some greyhounds Lodovico gave him by his bed to remind him of his uncle's kindness. God help those who put their trust in princes . . . and God preserve princes from women like Beatrice."

"You can't blame her," I said quickly. "She wasn't here, and I'm sure she knew nothing of it."

"Didn't she?" Atticus said slowly. "Bellincioni told me that one of Lodovico's servants, Da Corte, gave him a curious piece of information. Before we left for Alessandria, Beatrice was seen going towards Rosate's house, carrying a small sack, such as bankers use for carrying ducats. She came back, several hours later, without the sack. Rosate left to return to Pavia the next day."

There was a long, heavy silence.

"We must go to Pavia at once," Atticus said at last. "Can you be ready tomorrow morning at six? Bellincioni will have two horses waiting outside."

"But I can't go," I answered without daring to raise my eyes. "I promised Beatrice that I would go with them to Annona to m-m-meet King Charles."

I was stammering and scarlet under Atticus's steady gaze.

"You do fully understand the meaning of what I have just told you?" he said slowly.

"I don't know. Everybody says different things. How can I know what to believe anymore?" I began to cry.

Atticus looked at me coolly. "All those tears are only going to get you a red nose, no sympathy. For once, I am going to insist that you do as I say. I shall send word to the Duchess that you cannot come."

"There might have been another reason for her visit to Rosate, an innocent one," I said forlornly.

"Poor Catya, what dreams you have," he said, and I shuddered to hear his contempt.

He left me to sleep alone that night for the first time. My thoughts were very poor company. I knew too well what I had done. If we had not left Pavia, Gian could have been saved. Atticus would have stood between him and Rosate's "cure" unto death.

The strain at Pavia soon began to tell on us, as it had already on Bella. I was horrified at the change in her appearance. In two months she had shrunk to a skeleton. The creased grey robe that she wore every day hung from her thin shoulders as though there were no body beneath it.

She seemed happiest when we left her as we had found her on our arrival, sitting alone in the unlit hall, staring into the cold ashes of the fire. When she spoke, she fled from one subject to the next as though the words were enemies, driving her on in a high, brittle voice until she lost the thread that no one else could follow and wept in front of us, her face buried between her shaking hands.

At first, she would let me do nothing to help. Nothing was said, but I knew her reasons. One morning, when she came from Gian's room red-eyed and trembling after an all-night vigil, Atticus forced her to go out with him for a walk in the park. Bella shook her head violently at first.

"I dare not," she said. "I cannot leave Gian." She looked round the room nervously and whispered to us, "They're here, you know. Everywhere, waiting, waiting. I can hear them."

Atticus put a hand out towards her, but Bella turned and backed down the hall away from us.

"Trust us," Atticus said softly.

She looked back at him sadly. "I don't know if I can trust anybody, anymore. I am so afraid."

"Unless you want to make an orphan of your little child you must relax," Atticus said to her in a brisk, practical voice. "Caterina will sit with Gian."

Bella looked at me doubtfully, but she allowed Atticus to lead her out into the courtyard.

Gian turned towards the door eagerly as I came in, then lay back with a sigh. Fatigue and illness had taken the madness from his face. He looked like a sick child with his soft, wide eyes and close-cropped hair.

"I thought — it was a different footstep, you see. I hoped that it was the Duke, my uncle. Will he be here soon, Catya?"

"I'm sure he will, my lord," I said, sitting down on the stool by the window. Gian smiled and pointed to the dog sprawling at the foot of his bed. "He gave me that, you know," he said

proudly. "He is so good to me. I wish I could repay his kindness."

"I think you have already."

"What? By letting him be burdened with ruling Lombardy?
Oh no, you are wrong. He told me what a hard task it was.
It was for my sake that he did it all, to spare me the hardship.
I have led a very selfish life, you see, with none of the cares of
ruling to bother me."

He paused, staring at the ceiling. "I don't know why Bella
has always worried so much about it. Always harping on about
our position and how badly I was treated. *She* never tried to
understand my uncle's affection for me."

He turned, wincing at the pain of sudden movement.

"I keep my own cure under the bed, where she won't find it.
Can you reach it for me, Catya?"

I peered underneath, glad to have something to do, but I
looked doubtfully at the bottle. "That's a strange cure, my
lord. Are you allowed to drink this?"

He nodded. "Rosate gets it for me in the town, but I have to
keep it out of Bella's sight or she'd take it away from me. It
does help to deaden the pain a little. Please, Catya, give it to
me. I need it now. Please." His voice was querulous, and I
silently handed him the bottle, knowing that I was helping him
on his way to the grave.

I made my voice purposely cheerful, because I was very near
tears. "It reminds me of a story I once heard in Milan. Shall
I tell it to you, my lord?"

He nodded without taking his lips from the bottle.

"Well, once upon a time, there was a certain Bishop of
Arezzo. Like you, he was very ill, and all the physicians came
running to his bedside with every kind of medicine you can
imagine. Nobody gets more attention when he is ill than a rich

churchman. Well, the bishop was a wise man and he didn't believe in their panaceas, so he hid them all under his bed. When the doctors returned the next day, they all began to praise his miraculous recovery, each of them taking the credit for himself. The bishop heard them all out patiently, and then he showed them the untouched bottles and said, 'Well, gentlemen, and had I drunk your medicines, perhaps I should have become immortal?' "

Gian laughed. "How fortunate I am to be in Signor Rosate's hands, and not theirs! You're like Beatrice, Catya. She used to tell me stories all the time, but she never comes to see me now. Where is she?"

"At Annona, entertaining the French King and his court."

"Why aren't you with her, Catya?" he asked. I smiled at him. "I would rather be with you, my lord." I wished that there were any truth in that.

We both turned at the sound of voices in the courtyard, and I leant out the window to look. "I wonder who it is. I thought I heard the Duke's voice."

"I knew he would come," Gian said joyfully. "Now I know I shall get better. Go, Catya, quickly, and bring him to me."

I had to stop on the way down the stairs. Tears were blinding me, salting my lips and stinging my eyes.

The noise in the great courtyard was deafening. Soldiers were still riding in under the arch, many in unfamiliar uniform, whistling and wheeling their high-stepping horses on the cobbles. I picked my way through the crowd, blushing at the soldiers' comments and glances as I raised my skirt out of the muddy pools of water.

In the centre of the confusion I saw Lodovico talking to a small, ugly man whose face I did not know. The Duke looked tired and irritated. I curtsied to him, and he nodded brusquely.

"Where is the Duchess of Milan? The King of France has two hundred horses to be stabled, and his men are hungry. So are we, for that matter."

"Why, she's just . . ." I saw Bella coming out of the shadow of the arch, but she shook her head violently and ran back, out of sight. "She's gone out into the gardens, my lord. She will be back presently. I don't think she knew you were coming."

"I did not know myself until yesterday," said the Duke. "King Charles has expressed a desire to see his cousin, Gian."

The small man looked down at me and I dropped him a deep curtsey, soaking the hem of my dress. When I raised my eyes, I found that his were staring reflectively down at my breasts. I shook my hair forward to cover them, suddenly embarrassed. The King smiled.

"Another charming lady?" he said. "How wrong I was to think that all of Lombardy's beauties were gathered at Annona."

I fidgeted under his probing, humourless eyes. "I would have been there, too, sire, but since the Duke was so ill . . ."

I stopped in fright as I saw Lodovico's expression.

"Ill?" Charles said quickly. "We had no knowledge of this."

"A minor ailment. I did not think it necessary to worry you with such details." The Duke's voice was smooth.

"She said 'so ill,' and yet you speak of minor ailments? Curious, but how convenient for you if Gian's illness should prove fatal."

Charles frowned and flicked his fingers against the embroidered saddle.

"I think," he said with a small, cold smile, "I would prefer to see my cousin unaccompanied."

"He has been well looked after," the Duke said defensively. "Rosate, who diagnosed your . . . er . . . smallpox at Annona. An excellent physician."

The King smiled. "If his doctoring is equal to his diplomacy, I am bound to agree with you. What an invaluable man to have in your service."

The Duke looked at him uneasily. "Yes, he has proved helpful. Well, enough of that. Caterina, will you go and find the Duchess and tell her that she has a royal guest?"

"She is in her rooms," Atticus said. "Weeping."

"Perhaps the King can be of some assistance?"

"I always forget how innocent you are of the ways of the world," Atticus said. "If the King should happen on the truth, he will still do nothing about it. It will not suit his purpose. At the moment, Lodovico's support still has its uses to him."

"I do not think I like the King," I said, and told him of Charles's appraising glances.

"He probably wants to bed you," Atticus said calmly. "He is showing better taste than usual. From what I have seen of King Charles, he seems of no great value, either in body or mind."

"What shall I do?"

"You can hardly refuse a king. I am sure Beatrice would not," he said and turned away abruptly.

I caught him by the sleeve, forcing him to look at me. "Atticus, I thought you loved me. How can you speak like this?"

"Catya, Catya," he murmured against my hair as I clung to him. "Don't you understand? This has nothing to do with my love for you, but what good would it do us if I challenged the King for bedding my wife? He would only complain to Lodovico, who cares more for his French alliance than he does for your virtue. I love you, Catya, don't doubt that, but we are only pawns in a game of kings and queens. You yourself have reminded me often enough that we are dependent on the Baris. We are not our own."

"I am yours," I said, weeping.

Bella was sitting in her room, half-hidden behind a barrage of stools.

"I won't see him," she said as soon as she saw me. "They may eat and sleep here if they wish, but I cannot see the King. To think he is at this moment preparing to ravage Naples, to spill the blood of my family . . ."

"You must," I said, cutting off her rising voice. "The Duke has commanded it. Perhaps you could dissuade him from marching on Naples. He seems to have a weakness for women, but . . ." I looked at her stained dress and matted hair.

She sighed. "I know. I am not a fit sight for anyone. If you really think there is any hope, I will see him."

I didn't, but I redoubled my assurances in order to persuade her.

When she came into the hall an hour later, she had made a brave effort to resurrect the elegant, graceful woman she had once been, but all the rouge and silk in Lombardy could not have called up more than a parody of the past from her gaunt figure and thin, sallow face.

I saw the little King take a step backwards, his mouth dropping open. He recovered quickly and went forward to meet her, his hands outstretched. Bella dropped heavily to her knees in front of him, like an old woman.

I could not hear her low voice and the Duke hurried forward, fearing a betrayal. Bella did not look at him.

"Alone?" I heard the King say doubtfully. "Yes, if you feel it is necessary."

"You may say anything you wish before me, my dear," Lodovico said anxiously. Charles turned to face him.

"Your anxiety always to be present mystifies me," he said. "You have already imposed yourself, unasked, on my meeting

with my cousin, and now you seek to do it again. What makes
you so fearful, my friend?"

The Duke shrugged and turned away. There was nothing he
could say. Charles raised the Duchess to her feet. "We will
leave your uncle to speculate, madam," he said.

Lodovico stood beside me, listening to the retreating footsteps, and his long fingers plucked at his embroidered cloak.

"Is the Duchess coming to Pavia, my lord?" I asked.

"What? Oh, Beatrice. No. She is too much upset by the
Duke's illness," he said, a little too quickly. "She was so fond
of Gian."

"You speak of him in the past tense already?"

Lodovico brushed his hand across his eyes. "Rosate says that
he cannot live for more than a few days." He hesitated. "Tell
me, Catya, does the Duchess of Milan show any signs of . . . ?
Has there been talk of . . . ?"

I stood silent, making Lodovico look at me. After a while,
he continued. "Your husband's friend, Leonardo, has a peach
tree in his garden. I have heard that his experiments led him
to poison the fruit. You would not want to see your friend
accused of murder, Catya?"

I stared at him in amazement. I could think of nothing to
say. "No," I said at last.

The Duke patted my hand with an almost paternal friendli-
ness. "Then we will talk no more of poison, Catya. You see how
unwise it would be."

The door at the end of the hall opened and the King stood
there, framed against the light like a painted doll. Lodovico
turned to look at him.

"Well?" His voice was strained. The King came slowly down
the steps, without speaking.

"Poor lady," he sighed. "She begged me not to march on

Naples, but what can I do? God is on my side in this expedition, and I will not retreat."

"Until after you have conquered the south?" Lodovico said, anxiously.

The King shrugged. "Who knows? Italy is a fair land."

He gave Lodovico time to follow his meaning before he spoke again.

"I must leave for Piacenza tonight." He looked at me. "It would be delightful to have the honour of spending an hour in the company of such a delightful lady before I go."

I stared silently at Lodovico, willing him to save me, but he bowed and smiled as if he were the King's lackey.

"Go with the King, Caterina," he said, and turned to leave the room.

Charles took my arm and we walked sedately along, the maypole and the white rabbit. Not a word was said as we walked through the courtyard, but the King smiled and looked very well pleased. Resigned already, I wondered what he would choose for the scene of his attack.

"I would like to see the view from the upper rooms," Charles announced suddenly, and he forced my arm round with surprising strength until we were walking towards the staircase under the archway.

"Have you not admired it already, Sire?"

"I cannot gaze enough on the beauties of Pavia."

End of conversation.

"Tell me," Charles said. "Why did such an intelligent and beautiful woman marry such a dull man?"

It was difficult to control my anger and answer him in a calm voice. "I was unaware that you had met my husband, Sire."

"Not yours. I speak of your mistress. What a woman! Such charm! Such wit! She should be a Frenchwoman. Tell me the truth. Why were you not at Annona with her?"

"My duty lay here — with your cousin," I said.

"Oh, most proper."

Charles gave a yawn that he did not attempt to hide.

He did not even have the grace to find a bedroom, but took me up against the passage wall. It was a brief and passionless experience, devoid of preliminaries or pretence, a ritual that the King seemed to enjoy as little as I did. I did not see why I should simulate pleasure, and when he had finished, I pulled down my skirt and dusted it down as if nothing had happened. I noticed him writing something down and looked at him curiously.

"I like to keep count," Charles said. I flinched.

"Shall we rejoin the Duke, or would you like to admire the view that you spoke of?" I asked coldly. He had the grace to look ashamed.

The silence left behind after the King and Lodovico had gone their separate ways was even more forbidding than it had been before they came. The Duke of Milan's mother, the old Duchess of Savoy, arrived to weep noisily at Gian's bedside, and stayed. Her nervous garrulity was almost offensive, and I stayed out of her way. We went through the long days without speaking, for there was nothing left to do but wait.

Only Bella was with him when he died. She told us the news in a flat, small voice, and her eyes entreated us to say nothing. His body was so thin and wasted that it weighed no more than a child. There was metal in the pores of his skin.

The old Duchess rose in a rustle and tremor, and she clasped Bella's stiff, gaunt body to her.

"My poor child, what can we say? You have not deserved such suffering. Oh, my son . . ."

"Please don't," Bella said, gently disengaging herself. The Duchess went slowly back to her seat, sniffing and looking mortally offended. She would never understand. Bella came and sat down between Atticus and me, very straight in her high-backed chair, her hands clenched in her lap.

"We were very happy before this happened," she said, almost defiantly, and looked round at our faces. We nodded and she leant forward towards the empty fireplace. "He was beginning to change his ways. We had begun to go out riding together in the evenings, to take pleasure in each other's company. It was like the first year again. It was not — as people thought."

"I'm sure that is true," I said quickly, as her voice started to crack.

"What will you do now, Bella?" Atticus asked her gently. "Will you come with us to Milan?"

"To see Lodovico crowned?" she said. "I will deprive him of that pleasure, at least. No, I shall stay here with my children. This is my home."

"But you can't live here all alone, my dear," the Duchess of Savoy said in dismay. "Lodovico and Beatrice must give you a house in Milan. It is the very least they can do, in these circumstances."

"I do not want their charity," Bella replied.

We could do nothing to change her mind. She was inflexible in her pride.

I was in no mood to join the cheering crowds on the day that Lodovico was elected Duke. It was less than a week since Gian had died. I sat in the window with Giulia and watched in silence as the banners and brightly painted carts and carriages went past.

"Look!" Giulia craned forward for a better view. "There go the Duke and his wife." She sighed. "They do make a beautiful couple. She's a lovely young lady, always so smart in all the new fashions."

I turned away from the window to the dark room.

"Don't you want to see them?" She sounded shocked. "You won't get a better view than this."

"I must get on with some work," I said abruptly before she could open her mouth to give me one of her homilies.

Atticus came back from the cathedral alone.

"Well? Did it go smoothly?" I asked.

"There were two notes pinned to the pulpit accusing Lodovico of murder, but we removed them before he arrived. Otherwise, it all went according to plan. Beatrice came in for her usual quota of admiration, the people shouted 'Long live the Moor' as heartily as good citizens should, and the Duke seemed — nervous."

"And Beatrice?"

"Calm, collected, the perfect Duchess. After all, she has had three years to rehearse the role."

He lay back in his chair and I went to sit in his lap. He kissed me, but absent-mindedly. I stood up.

"What is it, Atticus? You are worried about something."

He shrugged. "Nothing new, but I cannot persuade either the Duke or the Duchess to listen to it."

"To what?"

He began to pace up and down the room, then suddenly stopped and turned to me.

"Have you never thought, Catya, that if Charles and Orleans defeat Naples, Orleans is in a very strong position to claim Milan?"

I looked at him, startled. "You think he will declare war on the Duke?"

"I am quite certain that he will. It is what he has always wanted, to possess Milan. And if the ducal expenditure continues at the present rate, we shall have no resources to defend the city."

"But you say that you have talked to the Baris — the Duke and Duchess of Milan, I mean — and they would not listen?"

He shook his head. "Why should they? Beatrice's pride is riding higher than ever now, and the Duke follows in her wake. All the Duke would say to me was that if there was any cause for worry, the Emperor Maximilian would help us! What a fantasy! He doesn't object to taking money from us, but when the coffers run dry, the Emperor would let Lodovico sink beneath the waves of his own disasters and never raise a finger to help. Still, they will find that out for themselves soon enough."

CHAPTER XI

ATTICUS'S FEARS were well founded, but it was clear that Lodovico and Beatrice were not prepared to listen to advice. They had enjoyed their new status as Duke and Duchess of Milan for two months, and already I was beginning to find them intolerable in their grandeur. I went with some reluctance to try again to persuade Beatrice to curb her extravagance, but she only laughed at me.

"You listen to your husband too much for your own good, Catya," she said. "You should be like me. Anyway, what do scholars know of politics? Isabella is arriving tomorrow to stay for Christmas, and I intend to send her away feeling chastened. You would not want her to pity me and think me poor, would you?

"Come, Catya," she said coaxingly, as I stood silently. "You were always my greatest supporter against my sister. You would not desert me now?"

I laughed unwillingly. "Well, perhaps not."

A slim, beautiful girl came in with a tray of sweet cakes. Beatrice began to demolish them, at a speed that astonished me. It was not surprising that her new fashion was for loosely cut dresses. She needed them.

"You have not met," she said, her mouth still full of cake. "Lucrezia Crivelli, my new waiting woman."

The girl smiled and curtsied. I did not like her face. It was exquisite in its way, but sharp, almost sly.

"Isabella sent her from Mantua," Beatrice said. "One of her more amiable gestures. Another was to make her husband stay behind while she comes to visit us. I could not have endured Gonzaga's company for more than a day."

She waved to me to come back as I started to leave the room.

"Tell Bella that she must come and join our party at Christmas. I think she is most unfriendly, hibernating in her rooms from morning to night."

"You can scarcely blame her for not seeking your company," I said in a low voice. "You know her reasons."

Beatrice ignored me. "Give her the message," was all she would say.

I met Sanseverino on his way into the Duchess's room. He looked startled.

"I thought Beatrice was alone?"

"She is, now."

I turned to watch him go in, heard the muffled laughter and walked away, wondering that Lodovico did not mind being made a cuckold so publicly. There was no one at the court who did not know of Beatrice's affair, and who did not laugh at the Duke's apparent ignorance.

With Isabella's arrival, the pace and grandeur of the parties in the private rooms of the Rochetta accelerated until I began to feel that we were sliding down a great golden chute to certain oblivion.

There was no doubt in anybody's mind that Beatrice was hugely enjoying flaunting her treasures, her clothes, her castle before her sister. Isabella was shown everything that was likely to impress her, from castles to Venetian mirrors, and she admired it all with the slow, feline smile that she had always used to hide her thoughts. She had good reason to smile. For all Beatrice's money and new clothes, she looked like an innkeeper's daughter beside her sister. The difference was now that she no longer noticed it. The Duke did. We all observed that he showed a marked preference for Isabella's company, and she had never been one to refuse admirers.

I liked Isabella better now that I was at a distance from her. It was easier to appreciate her wit and acumen when she could do me no harm. I admired her diplomacy in a difficult situation. If she felt envy or irritation, she showed no sign of it. She was loyal in public to Beatrice, as her sister.

I was surprised when she came into my room without warning one day. Luckily, Atticus was in the library at the Castello. He had disliked Isabella ever since their brief meeting at Beatrice's wedding.

"Caterina," she said, holding out her hand with easy grace. "May I sit down?"

"Of course."

"Lord, it's so peaceful here!"

Isabella sank back with a sigh. "It's worse than living in a zoo in the Rochetta, with that fool Bellincioni whining in one ear and Rosate yapping at the other. I don't know which of them I dislike more."

She began wandering round the room, picking up every object and examining it. I watched her nervously, remembering her acquisitive nature. She paused over the small drawing that Leonardo had given me.

"Clever Caterina to have such good taste in friends. I would like to be re-introduced to Signor Leonardo. Mantegna's portrait of me has been a great disappointment."

She turned towards me with a malicious smile. "I hear Leonardo won't paint my poor sister. She's put on weight, of course. Quite a plump little partridge nowadays, under those peacock clothes." She dropped each word clearly and finally in front of me, like a row of sharp pebbles. Briefly, my heart went out to Beatrice. All the effort she had made to impress Isabella, only to be written off as stout.

"Do you find her different otherwise?" I asked curiously.

The light fell across Isabella's face as she went over to the window to study the drawing.

"Different?" she said slowly. "Yes. She has changed more than I had realised from her letters. That was partly why I came here to see you. Warn her to be careful, Caterina."

She leant against a pillar and looked down at me. "She might listen to you. Tell her this. If she wants to keep her husband and her treasures, she had better change her tactics. She orders him about too much, and she is flaunting that pretty boy of hers too obviously. The Duke doesn't like it. Anyway, Sanseverino has a pretty wife of his own. Only eleven, too. Room to grow on him."

"Marriage never deterred you," I said dryly.

Isabella laughed. "You haven't changed, Caterina. Still sitting in judgment whenever you have the chance. We all have our lovers, but discretion must be used. God knows I have enough to put up with from my own husband, but at least he keeps his mistresses out of my sight. The only time I caught him out, I pulled the girl's hair out in chunks that thick." She pinched an inch of air in her slender fingers.

I burst out laughing at the thought of Isabella in the unlikely role of the jealous wife, but she did not react.

"I am perfectly serious, Caterina. If the Duke is provoked and made to feel Beatrice's inferior . . . She is not graceful with her power."

I looked up as the outer door slammed shut. Atticus burst into the room. He gave me a cursory nod.

"There's trouble. Charles has taken Naples, and the Duke has lost his nerve. Now that he sees Orleans will lay claim to Milan, he is preparing to drop the French alliance."

"Trouble indeed," Isabella said softly. "And where does the Duke contemplate looking for protection against his former friends of France?"

"Your sister has made the decision," Atticus said. "She is the ruler here, not the Duke. The plan is that we are to join all of France's enemies, if they will forgive us for having brought the French to Italy. If they will accept us, we shall be safe, for they are very powerful."

"I know." Isabella nodded. "Ferdinand of Spain, the Pope, the Emperor Maximilian and Venice. They all stand to lose by a French victory. Which is why they hate each other — and are in League."

Atticus looked at her admiringly. "It is an honour to talk with such a well-informed woman."

My mouth dropped open, but Isabella went on without bothering to look at me. "And what are their other plans?"

"Sanseverino's being put to work, undoing what he did. They're sending him to Asti with all our troops, as soon as the League have accepted us."

Isabella drew in her breath. "Sanseverino invading the town given to Orleans. That is bold."

I felt lost in the discussion. It didn't seem to me that Atticus hated Isabella at all. I ruffled my skirts and coughed.

"How did Charles win Naples so easily? Surely the King was prepared?"

Atticus turned from Isabella, reluctantly, I thought.

"It's a strange story. He never tried to fight. He has fled south to Sicily and the messengers say that he was like a madman, calling out that every tree was a Frenchman and declaring that the barons had come back to haunt him and drive him mad. Perhaps your father rose in revenge. Who knows? Well, Charles has left Italy in as sorry a state as we feared. Poor Piero de

Medici has been thrown out of Florence for good and Savonarola is threatening death to all Medici supporters."

"That's the seal of death on Florentine art," Isabella said reflectively. "I should have approached Botticelli before this new regime. If Savonarola has his way, all the paintings commissioned by Cosimo and Lorenzo will be destroyed."

Atticus exploded as soon as she had gone, much to my satisfaction.

"Really, she is an abominable woman! Does she think of nothing but acquiring paintings and people like a magpie? Beatrice is a saint in comparison."

"I was just thinking how much I liked her." I was too delighted at Atticus's reaction not to lie.

Atticus was not deceived. "I would be surprised if Isabella has many friends among her own sex," he said. "I would not trust her if I were a woman."

I smiled and said nothing, but I was pleased to see Isabella and her retinue return to Mantua.

I knew that Beatrice would be curious to know why Isabella had visited me. I had no doubt that she would have heard of it. There was nothing, however trivial, that was not reported back to the Duchess's private rooms.

Sanseverino was away from the court, laying siege to Asti, and Lodovico was dull company when he was afraid. So Beatrice sent for me to come hunting with her on the first fine day of spring. She did not begin to talk until we were outside the city wall, for there were her usual audience of admirers in the streets, and Beatrice always gave them the full benefit of her attention. That was why they loved her. She had been clever. The complaints in Milan were always against Lodovico, never her, and yet the extravagance was all Beatrice's.

We rode on down towards the soft, green plain where the rivers overran their banks and the trees' winter skeletons were all plumped out with blossom.

"Well," Beatrice said, "and what did Isabella have to say, Catya? Nothing good, I am sure."

"She is kinder than she used to be," I parried.

"That is no answer," Beatrice said, flicking at a low-hanging branch to loose a shower of leaves and flowers over our heads.

"We talked of general affairs."

"Did you indeed?" Beatrice smiled gently. My horse reared, nearly unseating me, as she brought her stick down with swift viciousness across its back.

"Now tell me," she said. "I will not have you playing games with me."

I looked at her profile, hard as marble against the light.

"She thought that *you* were playing at games that were too dangerous."

"I do not play games. Be more specific, Catya. I am most — intrigued."

"You won't be angry with me?"

She laughed. "You sound like poor Lodovico. He lives in terror of my rages." There was a smug undertone in her voice.

"That was one of Isabella's criticisms. She thinks that you should not rule the Duke so — obviously."

"But that is his choice," Beatrice said, reining in and opening her eyes to their widest extent. "You should have told her that. He relies on me to make his decisions. He likes to be left free of worry."

I edged my horse out of her reach on the other side of the narrow path before I answered her. "I think she meant that it is unwise to break him down instead of building him up. I have seen you doing it, Beatrice, so you cannot deny it. When he was so fearful about the French invasion, you were so hard that he seemed more afraid than ever."

"It is the only way to make him act," she said. "At the last resort, I cannot announce our plans. I can only suggest them. If I did not spur him on, he would do nothing. Look what the results of my efforts have been. Orleans will renounce his claim to Lombardy and we will take Asti. We always win, Catya."

And I, poor fool that I was, nodded and agreed with her.

I have always regretted my weakness that day. It was the last chance I was given to make Beatrice realise the danger of her power before the storm broke the following month. While Sanseverino took Asti, Orleans and the French counterattacked and captured one of Milan's most loyal supporting towns, Novara, where the citizens had at last grown weary of Lodovico and Beatrice's high-handed treatment. I was at court on the day the messenger brought the news. He was met by shocked silence.

"Taken over Novara?" Lodovico said incredulously. "But we were there last year. They like us well in Novara. You remember our visit there, my dear?"

He turned to his wife like a child for reassurance.

"What happened?" Beatrice curtly asked the kneeling messenger. "Surely they don't prefer French rule? If they do, they're a pack of fools."

"It would seem they do, my lady," the boy said uncomfortably. "The Orleans party had no difficulties. The gates were opened at once."

"Betrayal!" the Duke moaned. "I rule a nation of traitors. It is a judgment on us for our sins, Beatrice."

"No sins that I can recollect," she said firmly, but the Duke rose to his feet. "I don't feel well," he said. "I think I shall retire."

Beatrice looked silently after him, while the courtiers bent their heads or turned away, ashamed by Lodovico's cowardice.

"Well," Beatrice said coolly, looking down at us. "If my husband will not act, I will. Sanseverino!"

I looked at him, leaning against a pillar at the back of the room, his eyes half-closed. The courtiers parted respectfully before him as he sauntered up towards the dais. He was more arrogant than ever since his triumph at Asti, but he knelt before the throne. Beatrice's eyes softened as she looked down at him and she held out her hands. As they talked in low voices and life returned to the crowded room, I watched them together and understood. They were two of a kind, proud, vain and quick-witted as foxes, single-minded in their pursuit of power. Poor Bianca could never have been a rival to Beatrice, only a satellite. I wonder if she had ever understood the danger of her husband's friendship with her own stepmother. I saw her now, smiling towards them from her chair in the far corner. I looked again with sudden apprehension. She would have made a lily look like a country rose in comparison to her ashen, smiling face. She was only twelve, too young to know how to hide a breaking heart. For the first time, I condemned Beatrice.

I rose early the next morning and left Atticus still sleeping. He stirred as I pulled back the shutters to let in the pale sun, and I stood by the bed, watching him. His face was as gentle and trusting as a child's in sleep, half-hidden in the pillows, his hand curled beside his cheek. I pulled the cover down over his feet and crept out of the room.

Outside, the day was just beginning. The shopkeepers, sleep still in their eyes and slow movements, were at work already, letting down their shutters onto the wooden supports, turning them into trays for displaying their wares. Red-faced farmers' boys waved to me as they jogged past on their country carts, bringing in the day's produce and half the mud of Lombardy on their wheels. The first band of schoolchildren dashed past me, giggling as they nudged each other into the filthy gutters.

The Piazza del Castello was more crowded than I remembered seeing it since the day of our arrival. I passed a long-faced fishmonger sitting in the stocks, his face and body smothered and stinking with his own rotten fish, but for once the market women had left him to suffer in peace. The stalls stood unattended. Everybody was gathered in tight clusters around the clay cast of Leonardo's equestrian statue in the centre of the square. The proud, hawked face of Lodovico's *condottiere* father looked down at them as they screamed and chattered like starlings.

I took a deep breath and walked over to join them. Pushing my way into one of the groups with the help of my basket, I asked what all the excitement was about. One of them, a stout jolly woman who kept one of the stalls in the square, stared at me with her mouth stuck half-open in mid-sentence.

"Look for yourself," she said. I followed her eyes to the steady stream of troops marching into the Castello.

"It's been like that since dawn," she said.

"On the Duke's orders?"

She laughed loudly and nudged her neighbours. "Listen to the innocent! The Duke, indeed! We know what he's doing. Hiding in his rooms, the great coward, while his wife does his work. All he cares about is getting money out of us, so that he can impress his fine friends. If we are saved from the French, we know who to thank for it, and it isn't Lord High-and-Mighty."

The others nodded approvingly.

"My daughter works in the Castello," one of the older women said, pulling at my sleeve for attention. "She says the Duke is planning to leave us to fight for ourselves while he escapes to Spain and saves his skin."

"Disgusting, isn't it!" the fat woman exclaimed, her eyes still on the castle gate. She pointed, with sudden excitement. "Look! It's our Duchess, coming out from the castle. She's coming towards us."

They stopped talking and turned to look, wiping their eyes and shaking their heads as Beatrice rode across the square into the sunlight, her plumed hat nodding bravely. She halted in front of us, looked down at the curtseying women and gave me a small smile of recognition. If she was tired, she did not show it. Her voice was controlled, gently mocking.

"What fearful faces, my friends! Are you afraid to put your trust in me to save you?"

They stared up at her as though they were looking at the sun. One of the women ran forward and kissed her hem. Beatrice rested her hand on the woman's head for a moment and she came slowly back to join us, touching the place where the Duchess's hand had lain as though she had been blessed by a saint.

"We have sent to our allies from the League for help," Beatrice said quietly. "Everything is being done to protect you. So — you will not be afraid?"

They shook their heads, their eyes never leaving her face. She gave them a last gracious smile, wheeled her fretting horse away and trotted back across the square into the castle's shadow.

The promised help came from the League at the end of the weekend and the French stayed away from Milan. Orleans was biding his time within the walls of Novara, until he should be reinforced by King Charles and the rest of the French army in Naples. Apparently, the southern army was stricken by the plague and bad wine. We heard that they had decided to abandon the invasion and go home to France.

Beatrice was established as the heroine of Milan. The bells rang in her honour, preachers praised her in their sermons and she was applauded wherever she went. She seemed to have at last found the use to which power should be put, and I was happy to see her being rewarded by the love of her subjects. Now I knew all would be well.

A week had passed since my visit to the Castello square. I spent the day at home, helping Giulia to wash the linen and sweep the dirty rushes off the floors. She was too old to do it all, although she would never admit the truth to herself.

Atticus had been at the Castello all day, and when he returned, he semed silent and depressed. I waited for him to speak, but he patted my hand and disappeared into his study.

The light was still shining under the door of his room when I blew out the tallow candle in my room and went upstairs to bed. I lay waiting for an hour before I heard the door open. He undressed quickly and quietly in the dark and slid into bed.

After a little while I heard him sigh. I knew the best cure for sorrow, and I reached towards him in the darkness. It was a dark, quaking, shivering love that night, the best I have ever known, when I was the raped and he the silent ravisher and fantasy fused with fact. Afterwards, I lay in his arms while he stroked my face and body back to stillness.

"I will surprise you, Catya," he said suddenly. "For the first time that I can remember, my sympathies are entirely with Beatrice, not the Duke."

I laughed, well pleased. "Well, and what has brought this miracle about? Not my praises, I'll be bound."

"No, not that, Catya," Atticus said slowly. "First let me say that I admired her more than I can say last week during the panic. She was cool, collected, wise, everything that the Duke was not. The tragedy is that it has turned him against her. When I talked to him today, he could hardly say her name without starting into another flood of malice."

"But I thought he would be so proud of her."

"He is as jealous as a child," Atticus answered. "Now he resents her strength and popularity as much as he used to admire it."

He pushed back the coverings on the bed and started to pace up and down the room. I lay still, watching his shadow crossing the ceiling.

"She will fight to keep her power though, won't she?" I said. "I cannot imagine Beatrice letting herself be easily beaten."

Atticus shook his head. "Fighting will do her no good, now. She will have to take defeat gracefully, or . . . Catya, I was with him for almost five hours and he is completely inflexible. Apparently the final straw was when they went to the cathedral yesterday. He said that everybody in the streets was cheering Beatrice, but never him. He thinks that she has deliberately turned the people against him."

I raised myself on one elbow. "What does he expect? They despise him for being such a coward last week. First he sets himself up as some sort of god, and then they see him preparing to desert them at the first sign of danger. Why should they cheer him after that?"

"Oh, I agree with you. I am not saying that I approve of his behaviour. I am appalled by it. He told me of his future plans, and I hardly knew what to say. He is riding headlong into disaster now that he has taken the reins into his own hands."

I stared at him.

"Why, what are his plans?"

"Treachery, the natural policy of cowards," Atticus said scornfully. He sat down on the edge of the bed. "You must not repeat this to anyone, Catya. Promise me."

I put my hand in his. "I promise."

"The League want to capture King Charles," Atticus said in a low voice. "They have told the Duke that the French will be ambushed at Fornova, with the Marquis of Mantua leading the Italian army. The Duke is sending his own troops to help, but he has told Sanseverino to let the French escape. The horror is that he is delighted with his own ingenuity. He told me all this, and then waited for me to praise him."

"I don't understand," I said. "What good does it do him to help the French King now?"

"He thinks it will promote an understanding between Milan and France. He will always be able to fall back on it. It is useless, of course. The French will never trust Lodovico again, after his desertion from their side to the League."

"Does Beatrice know anything about this?" I asked.

"Nothing. She has no idea that the Duke has turned against her, yet."

I lay awake, long after Atticus had fallen asleep, wondering what I could do. And yet I knew it was too late. Lodovico could not let Beatrice threaten his power again, whatever the cost might be.

On the seventh of July a messenger brought the news of our defeat at Fornova, and the French escape. The court gathered to listen to the account in the Salotta Negra. The black walls enclosed us. The boy who brought the news was little more than a child. It must have been his first fight. He seemed like a trapped animal among the bright silks and sharp fox faces.

"We had bad luck from the start, my lord," he said in a low voice. "The river was high in the Taro valley and we were forced to cross lower down. Then the Venetians came down too early from the hills to attack the French camp and get the plunder from Naples. My Lord of Mantua fought bravely and urged us

on until his horse was slain under him. But then Count Sanseverino brought in the Milanese troops and . . ."

He faltered and stopped, looking around uncertainly.

"He, he didn't seem to know what he was doing. The Milanese
fell back and ran, so we were pushed back, and most of the
French escaped. Our men were mad with rage, with the King's
tent as their only prize of the day. They went through the valley
like wolves among the wounded and dying, hacking off their
legs and arms with axes and knives, anything that came to hand.
They say it was the bloodiest battle in our history. Four thousand dead in fifteen minutes."

And then, in the silence, Beatrice leant forward eagerly, her
eyes shining. "The contents of the King's tent? Do you recollect
what they were?"

The boy looked startled. The Duke looked away while
Beatrice waited with her eyes as bright as needles on the
messenger's face.

"Well? You have a tongue in your head, boy."

"The Marquis of Gonzaga took them back to Mantua for his
wife, my lady," the boy said slowly. "I did see them, though.
There was a sword and a helmet that had belonged to the
Emperor Charlemagne, one of the sacred thorns, some jewelled
crosses and a book of some of the — ladies that the King had
encountered in Italy."

"But they are mine, ours by right," Beatrice said angrily,
turning on Lodovico. "It is your duty to retrieve them and not
allow me, us to be so humiliated."

The Duke's voice would have warned anybody less foolhardy
than Beatrice not to pursue the matter. "They sound more to
your sister's taste, Beatrice. Do you not think it would be
more — graceful — to let the matter rest?"

"Remember where your loyalties lie," Beatrice said, her face
flushing. "Our men did not even fight."

The Duke shrugged, and rose. "So be it," he said. As he paused at the door I saw his eyes turn to the crowd, seeking somebody out. There were too many people for me to see where his gaze rested. I went away, wondering and fearful.

I was not pleased when I opened the door of our house one morning in early September to find Da Corte, now Chamberlain to the Duke, standing outside. With uneasy fascination, I had watched his quiet rise to power. A dangerous man to oppose, he was the Duke's spy — and he was said to dislike Beatrice.

"Well?" I said coldly.

"It's a message from the Duchess, madam. May I come in?"

He followed me into the room and leant back against the wall, whistling under his breath.

I read the note quickly, an invitation to dine with Beatrice alone in her private rooms that night. I hid my surprise, and held out the note. The Chamberlain ignored my outstretched hand.

"It's a pleasure to know the Duchess still has her friends, if you'll forgive my mentioning it," he said, smiling and rubbing his dry hands until they crackled like parchment. "I've always thought you had a good influence on her, she being such a headstrong lady. It's a dangerous thing to be too headstrong, don't you think — madam?"

"I was not aware that your opinion had been asked for," I said, turning my back on him.

"Oh, no offence, no offence. I meant nothing, of course."

He began to stroll around the room, assessing its contents with smiling, darting glances. Like a ferret.

"Very delightful," he said with a little bow. "You have done nicely for yourself, signora. I always thought you were a shrewd lady."

I looked at his velvet doublet, weighted down with gold braid. He smiled deprecatingly.

"I don't ask questions, and the Duke has been most generous, a very understanding gentleman."

Beatrice shrugged wearily when I commented on his familiarity.

"The Duke likes him, and my feelings are immaterial, now."

I avoided her eyes and looked down at my plate.

"Well, you must both be pleased about Fornova," I said brightly. "It is a great victory for Milan. Or should I say defeat?"

"They are the same," Beatrice said.

She looked ill, white even by candlelight. I noticed the fine cobweb of lines that had begun to net her face. She stared at me.

"I am worried, Catya, and there is nobody I can talk to about it, except you. Nobody with a mind of his own, that is."

"What about Sanseverino?"

Beatrice smiled. "He would perjure himself for a falcon, or a new choirboy. As a friend, I love him, but as a confidant, no. He tells Bianca everything and she, being only a child, repeats hearsay as truth." She paused. "It shocked me to find he was a party to my husband's treachery at Fornova. That shook my trust in him badly."

"Your sister, then?"

Beatrice pushed away her untouched plate. "No, not Isabella. I cannot admit defeat to her, of all people. You should know that. So I turn to you. Let us walk in the gardens. I am tired of this suffocating atmosphere, and it is easier to talk without light."

We left by the postern gate at the foot of the east staircase. The guards let us pass without question when Beatrice let her hood fall back.

Like a painted world the park lay in grey silence under the

pale crescent moon. Our shadows fused and crossed on the grass as we walked slowly under the trees.

Beatrice turned back to look at the windows of the Castello, yellow flares in the darkness. A silhouette pulled back a wooden shutter and the laughter and chatter slipped down the sleeping wind to where we stood, facing each other.

"What is it that is troubling you, Beatrice?" I said quietly, knowing I could not speak truths until she admitted her failure.

"I can't control him any longer," she answered. "I am afraid, and yet there is nothing I can do."

She leant back against a tree and stared up at the sky through the branches. I shivered in the cold wind, but she seemed impervious to it.

"The League know of Lodovico's treachery. They will send their army against us. Dear God, Gonzaga may lead it! Think. Milan may go to Mantua. My sister may be in my place."

"But your husband can turn back to the French. That's why he and Sanseverino let them escape at Fornova."

"Charles of France does not trust him either. Who would? He will let Orleans do as he wishes with Milan. He knows what a treacherous friend my husband is. Catya . . ." Her hands stretched out towards me in the darkness. "What can I do, feeling like this, knowing what must happen? You always knew what to do. Tell me now, for pity's sake, tell me!"

The darkness crept with sound. Wind on the water, wings in the rushes, and the sound of Beatrice's harsh sobs. Beatrice who never wept, crying because she knew that I had no answer to give.

Atticus and I went with everybody else to hear the Duke's speech, to show his new power. Standing on the cathedral steps in a plain suit of black velvet with his head thrown back against the wind, he looked more like a young chevalier than a middle-aged traitor. When he threw out his arms and said that he was acting for the deliverance of Italy, his audience was won. They needed to believe in him.

"We shall liberate the people of Italy from their chains and the glory of Milan and of our house shall be perpetuated forever," the Duke proclaimed above the roaring approval that was shaking the palace porticoes all round the square. "We intend to free Pisa from its Florentine shackles. And we will do it on our own. Milan shall rule in Italy . . ."

His voice was lost. "Moro! Moro! Viva Il Moro!" The old cry went up to drown the clanging bells in the church towers.

I should have liked to believe, but I no longer did. I looked at Atticus and shook my head.

It was hard to fight our way out of the square. Every little street was tight with people pushing forward towards the centre.

"Where are we going?" I shouted to Atticus, clinging to his sleeve.

"Where the wind takes us if the crowd doesn't break us first."

He turned down a black alley where the cats fled squalling before us to huddle like old women under the arches, willing us off their territory with blank yellow eyes. I leant back into the shadows as shutters snapped apart overhead. It is not good to walk in some parts of a city without an armed guard by your side.

"Oh, now I see where we are going," I exclaimed as I saw the golden curves of Santa Maria swelling over the roofs. "Sanctuary. Very appropriate."

There were muffled sounds of conversation at the far end of the church that stopped at the clatter of our feet on the nave. A small, round-faced man rose silently from behind one of the choirstalls and burst out laughing at our startled faces.

"Atticus Silvo, as I live! And since when were you a churchgoer?"

"It is less remarkable than your continuing survival of a novice's habit," retorted Atticus, laughing. "Catya, this is Signor Bandello, whose fondness for turning fiction into fact is making him the most notorious monk in Italy, excepting one."

Bandello's smile seemed ready to swallow his head. "Come, you praise me too highly, Atticus. My modest talents as a raconteur are only born of a wish to please, and if I embroider a little, it is only to enliven the story. Come up to the altar and help me rouse Leonardo from his lethargy."

Leonardo was silently contemplating his painting. I would have stood back and left him in peace, but Bandello showed no such respect for privacy. He trotted forward and patted the painter's shoulder.

"You've gazed on your masterpiece for long enough. Here are friends come to see you. Shall I fetch a bowl of wine? I have one waiting in the pew."

Leonardo shook off his hand impatiently. "It is only the face of Judas that continues to perplex me," he murmured. "I must find it."

"Why not use our beloved Prior?" Bandello said, grinning broadly. "He causes you enough irritation with his questions and criticisms. It would be an interesting repayment." He turned to us. "Leonardo sent our dear Prior into paroxysms of fury this morning by telling him that men of genius accomplish most when they work least. It actually silenced him."

"It is perfectly true," Leonardo said coolly. "When this is completed, the Prior will see that I spoke the truth. Well, Atticus, have you been listening to the Duke? I hear he is a changed man since he has shaken off the influence of his wife. Pastures new . . ."

"Meaning what?"

Leonardo took one of the brimming beakers from Bandello and stared into it reflectively.

"What a pity you were not at the dancing at the castle last night," he said suddenly. "I did all the choreography. Sanseverino danced like an angel. He makes the women look like farmers' daughters bringing home the hay."

"You're changing the subject."

"Not at all. I am approaching it with delicacy. There *is* a difference to a sensitive ear. Beatrice has some very pretty waiting women, don't you think?"

Atticus whistled under his breath. "So that's the way the wind blows. Which? Lucrezia Crivelli? She has a look of the late lamented Cecilia, now I come to think of it."

I saw Bandello look at them each in turn with sharp, quick glances, his smile gone.

Leonardo went on in his soft, deliberate voice. "The Duchess was absent last night. Sanseverino's wife was ill and since he would not forgo the dancing to look after her, Beatrice did. La Crivelli sat in her place all evening."

"I think you had better not repeat that story outside these walls," Atticus said slowly. "It would be unfortunate if the Duchess heard of it. Her pride has suffered enough as it is."

Leonardo glanced at Bandello, who in his turn studied the chrysalis colours of the fresco with excessive interest. The six eyes nailing his back brought him round to face us. He addressed his words to the marble floor.

"I think I did touch on the matter in my letter to Lady Beatrice's sister. Alas, the messenger left this morning."

"And you never thought she would make it the gossip of Mantua and bring it to Beatrice's eyes as soon as she dares?" I said angrily.

"It had occurred to me," Bandello answered, beginning to smile again.

Atticus took my arm gently. "I think we had better start for home, Catya, don't you?"

I turned to him after we had left the church. "Do you think that Lucrezia is a serious threat?"

"She is the type of woman who would appeal to Lodovico at the moment," he said. "The qualities you and I admire in Beatrice, her courage and tenacity, are those that the Duke most fears and resents. Lucrezia is more subtle."

I could find nobody to help Beatrice. She had made more enemies than friends at court with her overbearing manner, and now they were anxious to speed her downfall. They had no use for those who were not in the Duke's favour. Beatrice no longer had influence, and those who sought Lodovico's friendship paid court to Lucrezia Crivelli.

It was hard to tell how much Beatrice knew. I could only speculate. I did not dare to ask. She appeared unconscious of the bright, curious eyes of the court. Those who looked for tears and tantrums were disappointed. Only a slight change of manner betrayed her.

She was quieter now, seeking Lodovico's approval as he had once looked for hers. It was her idea that Cecilia Bergamini should be asked to the court, and I knew what pain it must have caused her. As a plot to divert Lodovico's attention, it failed. Cecilia joined Lucrezia's coterie, and Beatrice remained the outsider.

I was often with her during that cold, unhappy autumn of 1496. Her only other supporter, Bianca Sanseverino, was too ill to leave her bed, and the burden of companionship fell on me. It was a burden because Beatrice was too proud to talk of failure. The knowledge of it lay between us, making all conversation stilted and artificial. The first time she spoke of it to me was when we were sitting together in her rooms on a damp November afternoon. She had been silently twisting a skein of silk round her fingers, I remember, pulling at the thread until her skin turned white.

"Catya," she said suddenly, and stopped.

"Yes?"

"I received this today. Read it."

She held out a rolled sheet of paper, written, I saw at once, in her sister's hand. It was as spiteful a letter as six years of envy could make it. The opening was commonplace and predictable, an account of Isabella's appearance at a recent party, the compliments she had been paid and had accepted as her due. The reason for the letter came in the next paragraph: "I hope you will ever find it in your heart to forgive me for having sent you the little Crivelli girl. I hear she has caused rather more of a stir than you would wish for. Indeed, it seems that every court in Italy has heard of her success. I grow quite weary of the subject since nobody talks of any other. My friends tell me she is already being called the new queen of Milan . . ." And so it went on.

"Of course it is only her jealousy," I said.

"If Isabella knows, so does the world," she said in a small and miserable voice. "You do not know how strange it is to feel an exile at my own court."

Almost as though they had come to prove her point, a party of courtiers walked under the window, chattering and laughing but never looking up to where she sat watching. I heard another sound, running footsteps on the marble passage. "Someone coming to visit you," I said gaily, hoping that it was true. But it was a black-clad messenger with the news that Bianca Sanseverino was dead. I remember the white knots in Beatrice's hands as she clung to her chair.

"I thank you for bringing me the news," she said. "Has her father, the Duke, been informed?"

"Lord Lodovico was not in his rooms, my lady. I believe he has gone hunting with . . ."

"I do not wish to hear of his companion," Beatrice said quietly. I could see how hard she was fighting for control, and when the boy left she flung herself down on the sardonynx bed, sobbing into the embroidered pillows. I closed the shutters and sat still in the darkness, listening to her as she blamed herself over and over again. Picking up the fragments of sentences, I realized that although she held herself responsible, she could not admit the truth, that Bianca had died of a broken heart, knowing that Beatrice had taken Sanseverino from her. And now Beatrice, too, had been left to weep.

She raised her head to look at me. "It should have been I who died, not she."

"Stop it," I said briskly. "You have too much to live for to say such things. It is no fault of yours that Bianca died. Everybody knows how you cared for her all through this last year."

She shook her head. "I helped to bring about her death. We never should have given Sanseverino permission to consummate the marriage when she was so young. How could I have been so weak!"

Seeing no sign of an end to her tears, I went to sit by her, stroked her hair. "Why do you not organise something to take your mind away from worry?" I said gently. "There are the New Year celebrations to be arranged. Nobody else could do it so well as you."

"How can you expect me to put my mind to such frivolities now, Catya?" she said slowly. "Do I seem so heartless? No, I shall go every day to Bianca's tomb to pray for forgiveness."

"At least, let me come with you."

"As you wish, Catya, as you wish," she said indifferently.

And so it became an unspoken understanding that we would meet every afternoon to go to the church of Santa Maria. I was reminded of days that I had almost forgotten, kneeling beside my mother in the cold, deserted chapel at Maggiare, as I sat for hour after hour watching the winter sun streaking the great west windows of Santa Maria with gold, while Beatrice knelt like a statue of grief in the shadows. I knew that for her the church was a sanctuary. Here, she was watched only by the kindly, incurious eyes of the nuns who understood her need for escape, and said nothing.

Since the letter from Isabella, she had refused to talk of her worries. I hinted and alluded, but she was resolutely silent. At last I found the courage to broach the subject myself. Beatrice clenched her hands tightly, but her voice was controlled.

"I suppose everybody knows of it by now," she said.

"Well, rumors spread. You know how it is," I answered lamely.

"That is what hurts the most," Beatrice said softly. "Knowing that they are watching, waiting like vultures. Eyes that follow me everywhere. I only feel free of them when I am here."

"He will come back to you in the end, Beatrice," I said. "I'm sure he will get tired of her soon."

She laughed harshly. "Look at me, and be honest with yourself. Who would come back, seeing me now?"

She spread out her arms so that her velvet skirts tightened over her stomach, bloated with the child she was carrying.

"At least he still comes to your bed. That's a good sign, isn't it?"

"You're a fool, Catya," she said, without rancour. "You talk without knowledge of the facts. He hasn't touched me for six months." She put her hand on her belly. "This comes from one night when I went down on my knees and begged him to come to me. He came from pity, not desire. It is too late. Do you understand, Catya?"

She caught at my sleeve as I turned away. "Bellincioni has told me that he has their letters."

"You don't want to see them, surely?"

"I want to see the proof for myself," Beatrice said. "I must know where I stand, and their letters will tell me that clearly enough."

On our return to the Castello, I went to seek out Bellincioni. I knew where to look and only my present state of anxiety would have taken me down the cold, empty passages to Bella's private rooms. Bellincioni was the only person who visited her now. She never appeared in the court and guests were not made welcome in her rooms. I had hardly seen her since her arrival the year before. I knew that she had not forgiven my friendship with Beatrice.

I was puzzled. There was something strange about the small, heavily perfumed room in which she sat. I looked around it in silence, seeking the solution, and realised it lay in her arrangement of her possessions. Each of her bronze and marble statuettes had been turned to face the paintings and tapestries on the walls, their backs to the room. Bella smiled scornfully at my expression.

"I like them to share in my pleasure in art," she said. "Now I let them look on it all day."

I wondered if she had gone mad. "What an interesting idea," I murmured.

"Well, and what brings you here, so unexpectedly?"

Unasked, she meant.

"I was looking for Signor Bellincioni," I said.

He rose with the uncoiling smoothness of a snake from his artistic pose at Bella's feet. He gave me a small, cold bow. I

longed for an excuse to escape from the hostile atmosphere
that needed no sensitivity to discern.

"Beatrice tells me that you have some letters," I said quickly.
"I came to ask you not to show them to her. It would only hurt
her. It would be dangerous to upset her now, in her condition."

"It all depends on how persuasive she is," Bellincioni answered, smiling. Bella leant forward.

"Let her see them," she said fiercely to him. "You promised
me that. She shall suffer for her sins. It is the will of God."

"The will of God has nothing to do with it," I said angrily.
"She has suffered enough already, Bella. Are you so obsessed
with revenge that humanity means nothing to you?"

"Has she shown humanity to me?" Bella said. Bellincioni
nodded approvingly.

I tried to dissuade them, but it was hopeless. Bella had fed
on the past for too long, and Bellincioni had nourished her
hatred for Beatrice to the point where there could be no forgiveness.

I was very uneasy after I had left them. There was no more
I could do.

CHAPTER XII

SNOW FELL HEAVILY over the New Year, lacing the branches, padding the porticoes and streets. The excitement about the party in the Sforza Castello was infectious and I was looking forward to it more than I admitted to Atticus. I had a new dress with a high bodice and drooping sleeves of yellow silk slashed with scarlet. It was a little too tight for comfort, and I had to hold my breath and the bedpost while Giulia buttoned it up.

"It'll look better when you've lost a bit of weight," she said bluntly.

"It's fashionable to have the bodice tight," I said through my teeth.

"Not so tight as that, it isn't." I wondered why honesty is called a virtue as she looked me up and down disapprovingly. "Why don't you wear that velvet dress with the high neck? It's more ladylike."

I sighed. "I paid two hundred ducats for this dress, Giulia. I *want* to wear it." I smiled at her. "After all, one doesn't love a dress the less for having suffered in it." I got no answer to that and I swept out of the room, feeling victorious and not virtuous at all.

Atticus did not look up when I came into his study. "Look! Do you like it?" I fanned out the skirts and posed for admiration.

"Very pretty," he said, without looking up. I should have known better than to ask. He put away his papers and stood up with a groan. "Life would be tolerable if there were no such thing as society," he said sadly.

"We needn't go if you don't want to."

"And face your frowns and reproaches tomorrow? No, we will go, but I am afraid I am not looking forward to it with the same enthusiasm as you, Catya." He noticed the dress at last and laughed, putting his hand over the low bodice. "Is this for my benefit, or the spectators'? It's a very pretty fashion. I wish I could afford the jewellery that you should complement it with."

"Oh, I don't mind," I said lightly. "It's more original not to wear any."

"Dear Catya," he said, "I don't believe you, but bless you for saying it."

The party had started an hour ago and the streets were almost empty. The light from the castle windows reflected and glittered at our feet in the snow, while the occasional burst of music and chatter echoed towards us past the deserted loggias. I shivered suddenly.

"Cold?"

"No. A ghost on my grave. I was thinking of Beatrice."

"Very solid flesh for a ghost," Atticus said dryly.

There were crowds of people outside the castle, come to watch and wonder at the fine ladies of Lombardy or to gape at the armoured bodyguard who lined the way to the castle gate.

They were a remarkable collection, gathered from every country; Greek stradiots, Swiss lansquenets, and even some Scots archers looking very bleak and incongruous next to a band of dark Turkish guards. A party had arrived just before us and were standing chattering on the steps, forcing us to wait ignominiously at the bottom until they decided to move.

"They look so grand," I whispered to Atticus, and I clutched my little gold cross nervously. He slid an arm round my waist.

"Come on, Catya, where's your courage? They're like a party of peahens, those foolish ladies. Look at them, sizing each other up while they smile. Watch that fat one with her face falling because the girl in red has bigger emeralds round her neck. Their husbands are out to show the Duke that their coffers are as valuable as those in the Treasure House, and the ladies are so anxious not to appear provincial that they've succeeded in making themselves look more so than usual."

I began to laugh. "They heard you, Atticus. They must be furious."

The fat lady turned as I spoke and peered down the steps, saying in a tone of penetrating contempt, "Nobody that we would know," before sweeping her chattering flock up to the great wooden gates.

We were greeted at the entrance by an army of pretty pages in liveries of pink and blue with the Sforza-Visconti arms embroidered on their breasts. I saw Da Corte, the chamberlain, bustling to and fro behind them, shepherding truants into line, then rushing forward to bow and smirk at the grandest of the guests. Luckily, he didn't think we merited his attention.

I cannot remember the castle ever looking as beautiful as it did that night. We walked up the spiral staircase, where pages held willows of scented wax above our heads, up through the state rooms where the Sforza treasures were on display, none too modestly. "Like a merchant showing off his wares," Atticus muttered as we passed a marble table, creaking under the load of gold and silver. It was a slow journey. Those who had lived with the legend of the riches of the Sforzas stopped to stare in amazement at the rooms that I now took for granted; the Room of the White Doves, the Golden Room with its frescoes of past Dukes of Milan leading out their hunting parties to the fray, the Purple Room where the walls were hung with Lodovico's arms, embroidered in gold on crimson silk. I was more interested in looking at the ladies and the way they dressed. It was the one area over which Beatrice still ruled. Almost all of them had adopted her way of dressing their hair in two long plaits that hung almost to the floor, and most of them had plucked their eyebrows out of existence, which gave them a look of supercilious surprise.

"No, Catya," Atticus said, seeing me look speculative. "I can think of nothing more depressing than to be forced to live with an expression of constant amazement." A blast of trumpets drowned my answer. The doors of the Hall of the Pallmall opened and the guests poured through, like a spring flood at Maggiare.

Of all the rooms, this was my favourite, with its ceiling hanging above us like a midsummer night in a veil of golden stars and planets. The heavy scents of musk and ambergris were overpowered by the acrid swathes of laurel, ivy and juniper that Leonardo's assistants had looped between the windows. At the far end, the musicians were whispering and laughing on the high dais. I had heard that many of them had been brought especially from Flanders, and I looked at them with interest. Their faces were heavier and flatter than ours. They didn't look like my idea of musicians, but then they began to play, a Florentine piece, and the sound was so sweet, so perfect, that even the babble and confusion of conversations stopped for a moment.

I couldn't see anybody I knew, so I amused myself with watching the antics of society on its best behaviour. I never saw so many smiles for so little apparent reason. People seemed to put them on and off like masks, a defence against the unknown or unexpected. I soon realised that only a few of them knew their fellow guests. The smile was to disguise this, to show that they had friends and were not to be pitied, even the poor woman near us, hovering between three groups, belonging to none of them. I watched her stand alone on her little pinnacle of despair, unable to move, smiling and smiling with nobody to see or care.

Another group parted to release a butterfly, Lucrezia Crivelli, bold and beautiful in a dress of rose pink silk, cut so low that I regretted not having dropped my bodice another two inches. She passed close to me and I nudged Atticus who was deep in conversation with Merula, the Professor of Greek.

"Look! She's wearing the diamonds that Lodovico gave Beatrice at her wedding."

Atticus smiled apologetically at Merula. "You see the dangers of marriage. Talkative wives."

Merula nodded and leant towards me. "It is not wise, my dear, to voice such things here. Talk of nothing. No one can do that better than a clever woman."

"Except Leonardo," Atticus said, as the artist gracefully disengaged himself from the clutches of a determined lady of formidable size and came over to join us.

"Oh, I, too, have my troubles," he said with a mock-dramatic sigh. "This creature talks more than a cage of parakeets." He patted Salai's head, and the boy grinned at us as though he had been paid a compliment. I felt, as usual, rather awkward and embarrassed when confronted with Leonardo's inexplicable affection for him. It brought him down from a pedestal among the gods to our own level. Leonardo was laughing now, pulling Salai forward for our admiration. "The difference, alas, is that Giacomo's vanity is more expensive to satisfy than a cage of birds. As you see, he likes to play the courtier in Florentine velvet at a hundred ducats a yard, which I can ill afford."

"I like to look like a gentleman," Salai said sulkily.

"You may even carry conviction when your voice marries

your appearance," Leonardo said sharply. There was an uneasy pause while Salai glowered at his feet in silence. Atticus broke the tension. "Catya has been showing me the steps of the dances you choreographed, Leonardo. You've done very well. Will the Duchess Beatrice be leading them? I should imagine not, considering her condition."

Leonardo laughed. "You know her nature better than that. I managed to persuade her to join in the first set only, a very slow, sober dance that allows for her difficulty in movement. Our noble lord, ever tactful, suggested that Lucrezia should lead in the other dances."

Merula's face suddenly assumed the look of netted pain that I associated with his reaction to a particularly poor piece of Greek prose from one of his scholars.

"What is it?" I asked.

"Oh, nothing," he said hastily. "Will you forgive my leaving you . . . I've just remembered . . ." His voice trailed as he fled with unflattering speed. The reason was immediate and solid in the form of Signor Bellincioni, simpering along as innocently as a baby tiger towards us. His face was full of joy.

"I can promise you a drama tonight," he said. "I even dare to say it will be more lively than any of you, dear Signor Leonardo, could devise."

"How entertaining," Leonardo said coldly. "Come, Giacomo. We must not monopolise Signor Bellincioni."

The poet was quite unperturbed. He spoke to me in an undertone. "Watch the Duchess tonight."

I laughed. "Really, Signor, I find these extempore dramatics a trifle ridiculous. We're too old for children's games."

He was almost shaking. "I tell you, do as I say. I promise you, people will not laugh at Bellincioni after tonight. I may be only a humble poet, but even poets may play at being princes of power now and then."

"He's ridiculous," I said after he had sidled away to nudge himself into another group.

Atticus grinned. "He gets his just deserts. Since everyone knows that he measures his flatteries according to the presents he receives, his praises soon become as worthless as his insults."

The music stopped as he spoke, and as the great doors of the hall slid apart, the room was full of the quivering rustle of expectancy. Lodovico was too practiced in his appearances not to make as much use of suspense as an actor. As the ladies raised their heads from their curtsies to see what new fashion Beatrice was bringing to the court, they saw only two solemn pages, their trumpets raised like toy cannons to shoot the planets from the ceiling. Rehearsed to perfection in their minor roles, they bowed to their audience, then to each other and played a fanfare that made up in spirit what it lacked in merit. As they retired with military precision, Bellincioni strutted out through the door, grinning and bowing.

"I knew it," Atticus whispered to me. "Now prepare for half an hour of misery. Merula said that Lodovico and Beatrice aren't appearing until the exact hour ordained by Rosate."

The politeness of Bellincioni's audience was sorely tried. It is very hard to stand in the same position for thirty minutes with a look of polite interest fixed to your face like glue, especially in a dress so tight that every breath comes like a diver's gasp as he surfaces. To make matters worse, Bellincioni had plunged into such a morass of allegories that it was impossible to understand what he was talking about. I looked sideways at Atticus, but he had the look of rapt attention that I knew meant he was either working out some particularly complicated problem or wondering whether he could ask Lodovico for the salary still owing from last year.

For all the clashing of cymbals and braying of trumpets, the arrival of Lodovico and Beatrice was almost an anticlimax after such a long wait.

They were both wearing heavy mantles of gold brocade, lined with ermine, with trains that required six stout barons and chamberlains apiece to carry. Lodovico looked more like an emperor than a newly invested Duke, smiling with the gracious weariness of the mighty as he raised his hand in acknowledgment of his subjects' existence. I noticed two things. The ruby that had once belonged to poor dead Gian now blazed in the centre of the Duke's golden belt, and his eyes immediately sought out Lucrezia Crivelli. Pride did not suit the Duke. He was growing fat on it, and he had lost his easy grace of movement in a ponderous pace.

Beatrice looked like a ghost beside him, white-faced in a dress that stained her crimson, embroidered with white roses. The last signs of the girl had gone. I remembered Romano's bust of Beatrice five years ago, a round-cheeked child with her mouth curved up in a look of smiling uncertainty, not quite sure what was going to happen, who she would be. I had wondered then why he had left the eyes blank, unseeing, although Beatrice's had been full of vivacity and excitement. Now I thought I understood. Seeing that power would change her, he had no knowledge of what her eyes would reflect. If so, he had been right. Her face was thinner and older, but her eyes were the oldest and saddest of all. In a young woman of twenty-one they were unbearable. They still haunt me from that night. I shall never escape them. They are my indictment.

She stared without smiling at the crowded room and half-stumbled on the shallow steps. I saw Bellincioni rush forward to catch her. Instead of leaving her side, he bent to whisper to her. She smiled without gladness and nodded brusquely.

Their arrival was the signal for the banquet to begin. Atticus, sharper-sighted than I, noticed that Lodovico had placed himself between Lucrezia and Beatrice. "I would have thought it was rather unnecessary, unless he *wants* to cause gossip," he said mildly.

Sanseverino, on his way to sit at the high table, overheard him and paused.

"What do you think of the new queen of the castle?" he said, glancing at Lucrezia in her place of honour. "I think she'll make a charming Duchess. Don't you?" He looked sideways under his long eyelashes to see the effect of his remark. I laughed uncertainly.

"You aren't serious? As one of Beatrice's closest friends . . ." I left the sentence unfinished, remembering an earlier conversation with him. Sanseverino leant over my shoulder and I put my hand over my bodice in sudden embarrassment. I need not have worried.

His voice was smoother than silk. "May I offer you my advice, madam? Friendship is only another form of policy and it is no longer politic to be the *present* Duchess's friend."

I didn't answer. I was too angry. Sanseverino smiled gently and looked across the table.

"I'm right, am I not, Atticus?"

"Possibly. Politics seldom run the same course as our emotions."

Sanseverino laughed. "You should emulate your husband's diplomacy, my dear." He tapped my shoulder with steel fingers and was gone.

I hardly touched the food placed in front of me. Atticus offered me one of the small scented loaves decorated with silk flowers, but I shook my head violently.

"What makes men so cruel, Atticus?"

"Who?" He dug into a plate of peacock.

"The Duke. Humiliating Beatrice by flaunting that woman in public, in front of the whole of Lombardy."

"Keep your voice down, Catya. Listen." He looked at me sharply. "Don't forget that the cruelty lies on both sides. She tried to take away his manhood, and that, my dear, is a cardinal sin, whether it is done innocently or with intent."

I looked back at the Duke who had one arm out of sight behind Lucrezia's neck while Beatrice sat hunched in her chair, like a whipped animal. "You can hardly say that she's been very successful."

Our neighbours arrived and protocol forbade me to talk to Atticus any longer. I had done worse than he in the seating arrangement. He had been given Diana Pallavicini, a beautiful, treacherous girl, the sort that no woman likes and every man admires. She smiled sweetly at me and turned to Atticus. "Will your wife mind if I monopolise you? I've always hoped that one day I should have the chance of getting to know the famous Signor Silvo, of whom we all hear so much." Her voice was soft and too seductive. Atticus beamed at her. "Really?" I jabbed my fork into a Lombard cake as hard as if it had been her heart.

I had been placed between the most incongruous pair. On my left was Fracassa, Sanseverino's brother and the greatest bore at the court. Like the Marquis of Mantua, he could talk of nothing except fighting, and I can talk of anything else. I saw Atticus and Diana Pallavicini laughing behind their wine glasses as they listened to my despairing efforts at conversation. "What did he think of the Flemish musicians?" He didn't care for music. "Had he been to see Leonardo's fresco in Santa Maria?" He had never been interested in painting. Neither was he interested in travelling, poetry, the Church. I gave up in a flurry of frustration and turned to my other neighbour, Mariolo, the unofficial court jester. Poor man, it was not a profession of his own choosing, but he had been the victim of one of the ducal jokes two or three years ago, and Lodovico had never allowed him to forget it. As far as I can remember, he had gone hunting and mistaken a pet pig for the prey. People are very easily amused at court.

He chattered away, but I found it hard to concentrate when I could see Atticus gazing at Diana Pallavicini as though he were Adam and had just been presented with Eve. Mariolo picked up my thoughts.

"Your husband's a polite man. She's a very dull girl."

Reassured, I was charity itself. "She's extremely beautiful."

Mariolo grinned. "Never trust a woman when she praises one of her own sex. It's the danger signal. I've learnt that from experience."

"Which experience, more than any other?"

"From having lived in courts for three years. Courtiers have all the feminine vices to an exaggerated degree. They're vain, false, mercenary and as treacherous as a bed of snakes."

"Why do you stay here, feeling like that?"

He rubbed his nose thoughtfully. "I don't know, really. I used to be a soldier, but this has slowed me up too much for safety." He patted his large stomach with all the affection of the father of a naughty child. "So I sit around and I grouse a bit, drink a bit and talk a bit. You know how it is. We all complain that life treats us badly, plan new starts and feel a lot better for it, so we stay where we are."

He stopped suddenly and stared up at the table, his mouth dropping open to show me a masticated morsel of larks' tongues.

"Sorry," he said. "Country manners."

"What were you looking at?"

"The Duchess. She's cleared off. Taken offence about La Crivelli, I suppose."

He sounded unconcerned. I looked for Bellincioni and saw

that his place was empty. Atticus glanced at me and I knew that he, too, had noticed.

The rites of gluttony continued as ceremony unrolled. I went through the motions mechanically. Applaud the singers, eat, rinse away the smell of greed in rosewater, take clean napkin, knife and fork, smile, applaud the singers . . . some of the provincial guests had fallen quickly and quietly under the table to lie snoring with the dogs while the survivors grew louder and more raucous as wine overcame their manners. Fracassa, past the stages of oratory and overt aggression, was feigning to admire the stitching of my bodice so that he could run his hands over it. "Lovely girl, *lovely* girl," he intoned with the tedious repetition of the drunk. "You know that? You're a lovely girl." He made a sudden dive down my dress and I gave a savage stab with the point of my shoe under the table. Diana Pallavicini gave a cry of pain.

"Somebody kicked me!"

She stared at me accusingly and Atticus frowned. I was trapped. I could hardly say that I was trying to kick Fracassa, who had quickly withdrawn the incriminating hand. I glared back at Diana in martyred silence.

My eyes went back again and again to the high table. Lodovico, obviously the worse for wine, was feeding Lucrezia pieces of a marchpane Danae from his fingers while Sanseverino leant back and laughed. Bona of Savoy and Bella were sitting in frigid and disapproving silence, while the guests laughed and applauded, taking their cue from their host. He rose to his feet unsteadily and held up his glass.

"A toast, my friends, to the loveliest rose of them all . . ."

Sanseverino coughed, loudly. The Duke turned. "Yes, the loveliest rose of them all, the Duchess Beatrice," he said. Beatrice, standing silently at the top of the steps, stared at him as though they were on opposite sides of a precipice. She barely acknowledged the toast. She was paler than marble, but two scarlet spots flamed on her cheeks like the wounds of God and her mouth smiled.

Bellincioni had returned unobtrusively to his seat where he now crouched, looking rather unwell. I picked up my skirts and ran the length of the table.

"What have you done to make her look like that?" He edged away from me down the trestle.

"Answer me! What have you done?" I shook him by the shoulders. One of the guests began to make noises of protest and put a restraining hand on my arm. I pushed it away. Bellincioni mumbled something at the table.

"What?"

He looked at me dully. "I didn't think she'd take it so badly. I showed her the letters. She *asked* me to show them to her."

"Lucrezia's?"

Beatrice's high voice cut across his answer.

"Let the dancing begin." The guests applauded loudly to hide their embarrassment. I saw Lucrezia look at the Duke. She was frightened. She must have realised what had happened. Slowly she walked to her place in the arena, opposite Beatrice. The rest of us were superfluous, for all eyes were fixed on Beatrice. Nobody knew quite what to expect.

The band of musicians struck up and Beatrice's feet began to move, faster and faster until the rosettes on her shoes whirled like spinning wheels. The round faces of the Flemish players started to sweat as they tried to keep up with her. The slow beat of the dance had increased to the uncontrollable, hysterical speed of a tarantella.

I danced clumsily, forgetting the complications of the steps as I watched Beatrice. Her eyes were fixed unwaveringly on the pretty, frightened face of her rival and she grasped her hand in a vice of steel. Lucrezia was swaying and stumbling. I wondered if she was going to faint, be sick or both.

The laughter at the tables had stopped. Even the most far gone of the guests had realised that something was wrong as we spun and turned, puppets jerking in the power of something more powerful than we.

The applause at the end of the dance was forced, uncertain. No one knew what was happening. I walked back to my place in silence. Sweat was pouring down my face and I was too tired even to raise my hand to wipe it away. Fracassa had joined his kind beneath the table and Leonardo was sitting in his place, white and furious. Even his beard trembled with emotion.

"She ruined it, simply ruined it," he said bitterly. "All those weeks of practice, wasted. Has she no understanding of rhythm or does she want to turn the evening into a peasant get-together?"

In a whisper, I told him what had happened, knowing that his hatred of Bellincioni outweighed his dislike of Beatrice. He was, or appeared to be, horrified.

"Forgive me. I really had no idea. Only somebody of the insensitivity of Bellincioni could have done such a barbarous thing."

"I thought the Duchess was only going to lead the first dance." Atticus had been watching the next dancers taking their places.

"That's right. Why?" Leonardo broke off as we saw the answer. Lucrezia had gone back to the table. "Surely she isn't taking her place? It'll kill her if she keeps up that pace."

"Perhaps that's what she wants," I said and looked at them in sudden fear. They only shook their heads.

With the rest of the court we watched in stricken silence as Beatrice danced on, and on. The musicians were exhausted, but they did not dare to let the pace flag behind the command of the Duchess's feet. She allowed the speed to slow when she danced The Cruel Sort with Sanseverino. Under any circumstances, it was shocking that she should do this; tonight I was sure she was doing it deliberately. Of all dances, this is the one most meant for lovers, with its slow languorous movements and sweet, sad music. It stripped Beatrice's misery naked. She went through the slow parody of flirtation with him in a way that made my blood run cold. No one would have questioned that she danced it brilliantly, but the mockery of it was awful. Her eyes were cold with pain as she smiled coquettishly at her partner, feigned embraces, held his silk slipper to her heart, then dropped it at his feet.

The Duke was ashen. He had not touched his glass of wine and he stared at his wife as if he saw her for the first time.

The candles were guttering and spluttering on the tables and half the guests were asleep on the table, but the dancing still went on. The Dance of the Torches was announced and Beatrice spoke in a low voice to one of the Flemish musicians.

"The Duchess wishes to announce that she will take the part of the Angel of Death. Your places, ladies and gentlemen."

"Oh, my dear Lord," Atticus said under his breath. I clung to his hand as if it were a lifeline.

It was a strange experience in the slow darkness to watch the group of girls, like virgin guardians of the temple, weaving round Beatrice with their torches flaring in the blackness. The central figure, she held her torch higher than the rest and began to turn slowly at first, then faster as the dancers simulated exhaustion and death approached. She bent her light over each of them and they sank to lie like sleeping swans around her. Now she stood alone, turning in the emptiness. There was an odd little sound, like a choke or a laugh, and the last torch was gone.

Silence. Then a confused babble. The Duke was the first to reach her body.

Lodovico knelt on the wooden floor with his back to us, hiding her dead stillness, then slowly stood up.

"Rosate? The Duchess must be taken to her rooms. She is . . . not well." We all noticed the hesitation.

The doctor hurried forward, bent down and ran his hand with rapid expertise over her wrist. He spoke in a low voice to the Duke who nodded and turned to face our silence. His voice was low, but controlled.

"Forgive this interruption, my friends. If you would care to go through to the next room, I believe Signor Leonardo has arranged a mechanical entertainment. I will join you shortly."

Beatrice was carried out on the skinny shoulders of four of the pages, followed by the Duke, and the golden doors closed upon them.

The room returned to an echo of life as we obediently filed back into the Hall of the Pallmall. I watched the jostling crowd as if through glass, seeing but not hearing. I was numb and cold with shock, and I leant against Atticus for fear of falling.

"God, the coolness of the man," he murmured. "Can nothing disturb his sense of ceremony?"

"Do you think she'll recover?" My teeth were chattering so much that I could hardly get the words out. He did not answer, and my fear increased.

The room was plunged into darkness as we took our seats. We waited. Nobody spoke. The Duke came in silently. His face told us nothing. He sat, staring with every appearance of interest at Leonardo's set piece.

It was a very pretty contrivance, although nobody was in the mood to appreciate it. Musical globes revolved in front of us, throwing a spectrum of colour across the ceiling, and a golden-haired boy dressed as an angel recited a poem to the Duke, declaring him to be the monarch of all the spheres. Except death, I thought. Since there was no other way to show our sympathy, the cheers and clapping were long and loud.

The party came to an end at last. Lodovico had shaken the hands of most of the guests, cutting off all questions. The last carriages had rattled their way home through the dark, quiet streets. The candles had been blown out, the banquet cleared away.

Atticus and I sat by the fire in the Salotta Negra, waiting with Sanseverino whose false tears sickened me.

"My dearest friend, the only true one I ever had and the best woman I ever knew."

"Your *policy* seems to have changed, Signor."

"I don't understand you, Caterina." His tears fell steadily, but his eyes were as hard as agate.

"I mean that you said it was no longer politic to be the Duchess's friend. Is your memory so short?" I was startled by the harshness of my own voice.

His face warmed to his words in the firelight. "I spoke in jest, of course. You will vouchsafe for me, Atticus. It was only a joke."

"I understand perfectly," Atticus said slowly. "You're a shrewder fool than I mistook you for."

Sanseverino hesitated, only for a second. "I'll be frank with you," he said. "We all have to survive. If she dies, the Duke will remember only that he loved her, and I shall not be the first to remind him of the truth."

"Since we are being honest, it hadn't occurred to me that you would." Atticus's voice was dry with dislike.

They were both asleep in their chairs when the Duke came in.

"Well?"

"You should go home, my dear," he said so gently that I almost wept.

"I must stay," I said.

"Dear Catya." He put a hand on my shoulder. "Pray God she'll live. I shall be lost without her."

I looked at his white, strained face and believed him.

Rosate came in with the grey light of morning. "She is asking for you."

"For me?" I asked.

He nodded. "The Duchess Bella has only just left her. You must remember to be quiet. Don't strain her in any way."

The room was dark, stifling behind the heavy curtains. Beatrice was still, too still, in her bed. Whiter than the pillows and tears ran down her pale cheeks from closed eyes. I took her cold hand and pressed it.

"It is I, Beatrice. Caterina."

"Catya," she said slowly and opened her eyes. I expected peace and saw only pain. "I don't want to die. I'm not going to, am I, Catya?"

I shook my head and tried to smile. "She's dead, my new baby. He took her away from me without saying anything, so I knew."

"I'm sorry."

Now she clung to my fingers like a child. "We'll go to Vigevano when I'm better, just you and me . . . like the old days, feed the swans and we'll take the boat out to the island and have picnics every day . . ."

"Lie with our heads in the grass . . ."

"And watch the clouds. Lodovico would like that . . . he loves Vigevano." Her voice was so small and slow that I could hardly hear her. She smiled drowsily.

"Pull back the curtains, Catya. We'll watch the sun coming up."

The gardens still slept under the snow, diamond hard and still, while fat birds bounced and sank on the surface in search of food. I turned away from the window.

"Can you see? The sun's still down behind the trees." She tried to raise her head.

"I want to tell you something," she whispered.

I leant over her.

"When Gian died, I . . . I didn't . . . I'm so sleepy, Catya, so tired." Her voice slipped away as she fell back.

I made myself touch her pulse. Nothing. Nothing at all. I crossed her hands on her breasts, closed the lids of her eyes and put a flower, orange-blossom I think it was, from my headdress, between her small, stiff fingers. Then I knelt by the bed and cried while the pale sun climbed over the trees.

Lodovico rose as I came slowly through the doors.

"How is she?" He saw my expression. "She's . . . ?"

I could not speak for tears.

"Oh, God," he said softly. "Oh, God of little mercy." He hid his face between his hands, but whether he prayed or wept I could not tell.

Rosate touched him tentatively.

"My lord, we must . . ."

"Leave me alone," Lodovico said without raising his head. Rosate swallowed and tried again.

"We must make arrangements. The announcement, the funeral, all these things."

Lodovico sighed. "Make the arrangements for me, but let them fit her rank. I want no cost spared. She would like that. Also, I wish to see nobody, absolutely nobody between now and the funeral. I don't think I could bear it."

He stood up slowly, like an old man, and left us.

The Duke's hand was evident in the funeral arrangements. It would have been unlike him not to take an interest in its organisation down to the last detail.

People followed the funeral cortege in hundreds, weeping or with silent, hooded heads bent as we walked slowly past the houses draped in black under the dark winter sky.

There were more candles in Santa Maria than I had ever seen. The nobles, merchants, townsmen and everybody who had loved Beatrice for her youth and her brave gaiety, had brought offerings to the church and I was glad of it. She would have been pleased.

Her father, Ercole, had come from Ferrara, a long, hard journey for an old man. There was a moment's unease when Lodovico came down the aisle to greet him, his hands outstretched. Ercole looked him up and down with cold disdain, pulled his cloak tighter round his body, and swept past the Duke to his place as though they had never met.

Atticus wisely took me home before her body was finally lowered into its marble prison, for tears were pouring down my face so fast that I could see only through a mist and my breath came in sobs.

I could do nothing right and he was so kind to me. I dropped everything, I forgot what I meant to be doing as soon as I began it, my fingers shook as though I had the palsy. I wanted to see nobody.

About a week after the funeral Atticus came into the room where I sat, staring through the window at the clouds straggling like torn veils over the roofs.

"Bella is here to see you, my dear."

"I don't want to see her. Tell her I'm ill."

He put his arms round me, very lightly. "Catya, you must

stop thinking about it. Weeping and not eating are no solution. There never is an answer, only the continuation of life."

"I'll see her then, if you want me to," I said wearily.

She was sitting waiting in the hall when I came down the stairs. She held out her hands towards me. I put both of mine behind my back, like a child. "What brings you here, Bella?"

"I must talk to you," she said, looking at Atticus. He took the hint and disappeared.

"You made Bellincioni give her the letters," I said. "You made her seek death."

"I wanted to tell you how sorry I am." She looked at the ground while I sat, watching her in hostile silence. "I saw her that night, just before she died."

"I know."

"She told me — and I believed her — that Rosate and Lodovico told her that Gian was suffering from an incurable disease, and that the . . . poison was only to shorten his life by a few months, a year perhaps. It was still a wicked act, but she was very young. Worse things have been done, God knows. Her worst crime was her thoughtlessness. It was only that that made her cruel and she suffered for it in the end, poor child."

There was a long silence. "It must have been hard for you to say that," I said.

"Yes," she said simply. She looked up at me. "I also came here because I have a favour to ask of you. I know that Lodovico is fond of you and will listen to you. He has asked me to leave my rooms in the Castello and take up residence in the old palace on Cathedral Square. I am forbidden to take my son with me."

"He's sending you to that morgue? He can't be so cruel. You'll freeze to death there. Better that you live here with us."

She laughed bitterly. "And yoke you to my position and all that goes with it, including fifteen pages and three cooks?

I would never inflict such a nightmare on you, but if you could ask the Duke . . ."

"I'll try to persuade him, I promise you."

Her cold, dry lips brushed my cheek.

"We are friends again, then?"

"Of course."

What else could I say? I doubted that her mood of forgiveness towards the dead or the living would last. It was not in her nature.

I went to see Lodovico the next day. It was strange to find the huge state rooms deserted. The musicians' instruments were lying, untouched, on the dais. The chairs and tables had been pushed back into neat rows against the walls, and the tapestries and frescoes were hidden behind hangings of black velvet. No sound, only the echo of my footsteps.

In the long passages small groups of courtiers dressed in black huddled like penitents, talking in low whispers. They looked up eagerly as I passed, desperate for any diversion to fill the slow pace of the days. I pitied them, bewildered and lost without the entertainments that were their daily bread.

The Duke's rooms were empty, the curtains drawn. I went back to the Salotta Negra, where Beatrice's waiting women bent over their embroidery in silence.

"Where can I find the Duke?"

They looked up, startled. "Don't talk so loudly."

"Why not?"

"It's not allowed," one of them said in a whisper, and the others nodded wisely. I sighed and repeated the question in a low voice.

"We don't know. Nobody has seen him since the funeral."

At that moment, I saw Rosate walking past the far door and

I ran towards him, a volley of disapproval from the ladies sounding behind the clatter of my heels.

"Signor, please! Signor Rosate!"

He turned with a frown. "Don't you know that it has been forbidden to shout? Restrain yourself, madam."

"I must see the Duke."

"He won't see you," Rosate said with finality and turned to walk away. I caught at his arm.

"How can you be so certain?"

Rosate spoke slowly, as if to a very stupid child. "He has consented to see only the ambassadors from Ferrara, from the French court and from Mantua, and now you expect him to make an exception of you?"

"I would at least like to make the attempt." I was still clutching at his jacket. He pressed the fingers of both hands against each other and looked at me over the top of them through half-shut eyes, assessing my degree of persistence. I stared back at him, more determined every moment, hating his smile of weary condescension. He brought his palms smartly together with a crack. I jumped.

"Follow this passage, turn to the right, through the arch, left . . ."

He was rattling through it at a speed that was almost impossible to follow, on purpose, I think. I nourished my hatred with loving relish all the way down the passage, and felt better for it.

It took me a long time to find the room. I knocked timidly. I heard the restless pacing of the Duke come to a halt.

"I've told you, I wish to see nobody."

"It's me, my lord, Caterina Silvo."

There was a pause. I listened.

"Alone?"

"Yes, my lord."

The footsteps were coming closer now. The Duke opened the door.

The room was so dark that I found it difficult to see my way. He made an apologetic gesture.

"I prefer darkness. It soothes me."

I looked at his suit of rough cloth, torn and rumpled. He gave me an embarrassed smile.

"I'm afraid that the tears were inflicted by my tailor, not myself."

"Oh." I looked away.

"Have you been to Santa Maria? I hear the poor child's tomb looks well. I asked for it to be placed next to . . . hers." He spoke with a quiet devotion that moved me very much.

"I composed the inscription myself." He coughed. " 'Unfortunate child, I died before seeing the light: More unfortunate still, my death deprived my mother of her life and my father of his consort. With such a bitter destiny I have this one consolation — I was sent into this world by parents almost divine.' "

He looked at me expectantly.

"It's very poetic," I said lamely. Divinity seemed rather a large claim for himself and Beatrice. He nodded, pleased, and took my hands in his.

"How shall I manage to live without her, Caterina?" he said softly. "She, who was the light of my days, who brought me youth, happiness to my city, the lily of my court, queen among all women." Tears were rolling down his face. I pushed Cecilia and Lucrezia firmly from my mind and pressed his hand.

"I shall always remain faithful to her dear memory," the Duke said earnestly, "and Milan shall be renowned for the peace and serenity that *she* would have wished. No more wars, nor poverty. Think, Caterina, there are people in Milan who cannot afford to buy a loaf of bread. I shall personally see that the coffers of the Treasure House are distributed among the poor and hungry. No man shall want for wages or go short of good . . ."

"Bella came to see me," I said, as the Duke paused. "She is very unhappy that she must go from the castle and leave her little son behind." Lodovico hesitated, frowning.

"I am selfish. I will admit it to you. She reminds me too much of my beloved wife. Beatrice was so devoted to her."

"But she wasn't," I heard myself say. "You know she didn't like Bella."

The Duke withdrew his hand.

"Your memory betrays you, Caterina. Beatrice was never too busy to help her cousin. She loved her like a sister."

"What about the little Duke?" I persisted. "Bella said that you want to keep him apart from her."

"Not at all. She will visit him once a week. You may be sure he will be well looked after."

"But why can she not keep him with her?"

He sighed. "You are too innocent in the ways of the world, Caterina. Bella is a very difficult woman. She has been making a habit of taking her son out for rides in the city, and reports have come to my ears that some people were actually calling out to him as the little Duke, the heir to Milan. Now, you will see that the situation might become awkward if it were allowed to continue. We must remember Beatrice's child."

"Yes. I can see that."

"You're a good girl, Caterina," the Duke said, patting me briskly on the shoulder. "Very quick."

I found myself standing on the other side of the door without knowing quite how I had arrived there.

"Well," Atticus said as I came in. "How did it go?"

I pulled off my hat and sat down in front of the fire. "It was very sad. I never realized how much he really loved her. He was crying when he talked about her."

"Spare me the repentance," he said dryly.

"Don't be so hard, Atticus. He's going to give away his money, pay all his debts, reform the taxes . . ."

"I'll believe that when it happens. Nobody has better intentions than a man with a guilty conscience. He uses them to ease the guilt, and when they've done their work, they're conveniently forgotten. Did you get an answer about Bella?"

"Not in so many words, no." I avoided his eyes.

"Not even an intention?"

"You're laughing at me!"

"Am I?" Atticus said. I looked at his grey, unsmiling face and shook my head.

"The changes sorrow works on men are the most transient of them all," he said slowly. "Perhaps tomorrow we'll need the diplomacy of joy. Then Beatrice will be the scapegoat, not the saint."

"I miss her still," I said.

"I know. You were the only friend she spurned and never lost. And now she has you forever."

"Forever," I repeated.

EPILOGUE

WE LEANT OVER the narrow parapet and looked down into the shadowed well of the courtyard. My little Beatrice was stumbling along the edge, clinging to the pillars for support as she tripped over the hem of her long child's dress. She laughed and held up her arms as she tried to catch a scarlet butterfly, but it flew away over her head towards the sun and she looked sadly after it, her finger in her mouth, her eyes round and puzzled.

I called down to her, but as she looked up towards us she lost her balance and fell over backwards on the stone. I saw her face pucker up and I turned to Bella quickly.

"I must go down and see if she is hurt." Bella shook her head disapprovingly. "You worry too much. Look, her nurse is coming to fetch her."

"But she needs *me*."

Bella put an arm round my waist and drew me close to her.

"She does not need you any more than her namesake did, Catya. You are too obsessive about her. It will only frighten the child."

She hesitated and glanced at me. "You must not think you have re-created Beatrice. It is a dangerous game to play."

"She is very like her," I said eagerly. "I can remember Beatrice chasing butterflies through a field at Ferrara in just the same way."

Bella sighed and dropped her arm. "All children chase birds

and butterflies; there is nothing remarkable in that. You should be thankful that she has your looks and Atticus's tenacity, but still to be clinging to thoughts of Beatrice ten years after her death, that is ridiculous."

"You will never understand," I said wearily and leant back against the wall.

Bella looked through the window. "Our horses are here," she said. "We are going riding this afternoon."

"Oh. Where?"

She smiled and led the way out of the room.

I was puzzled. Bella never made a suggestion without good reason, but she was inexorably silent as we rode out from the castle. When I pressed her to tell me our destination, she laughed at me for being too inquisitive.

She reined in on the hilltop and looked down to the white and red city coiling round the silver bay.

"I shall never regret having come home," she murmured to herself.

"Even to live under the Spaniards?"

"Better to be in Spanish Naples than under the Sforzas at Milan," she answered quickly. "You are not sorry that we came back, are you?"

I looked at the bleak, fortressed walls of the Castel dell'Ovo and turned my horse away.

"Well?"

I shrugged. "There was no alternative. I could never have stayed for long in Milan after Atticus's death."

"Do you feel able to talk about it yet?" Bella asked in her soft voice as we rode down into the sleeping hills.

I blinked as the curves of the fields lost their sharp edges.

"It is foolish of me to mind so much, isn't it? I know it is what everybody says, but I didn't realise how much I had loved him until after he was dead."

She nodded. "I felt the same when Gian died."

I looked down at my hands, clenched round the silk reins. "As you know, it was in the first riots, two years after Beatrice died. You remember, when Lodovico fled to the Emperor for safety in the Tyrol and the French came into the city after pillaging Pavia."

"And Da Corte gave the Castello to the French instead of defending it. I remember."

"We were at home. Atticus had put me to bed because I was feeling ill. It was just before my Beatrice was born. He came into my room an hour or so later, very worried because he had heard that the mobs were out and Landriano had been shot in the rioting. You know what friends they were. Atticus insisted on going to see if he could find the body and bring it back safely. I begged him not to go, Bella. I remember clinging to his arm, crying until the tears drenched his sleeve, but it was no use. That was the last time I saw him alive."

I could feel the sobs cracking and tearing in my throat and I could not speak. Bella bent her head and waited.

"Giulia, the maid, and I sat up all night waiting," I went on, "but he never came back. They left his body on the doorstep the next afternoon, with a Lombard arrow in his throat."

Neither of us spoke. I could not, but as we rode on into the sun, I looked around me, half-remembering. "Bella, I know this path. Tell me where you are taking me."

"I do not need to tell you, Catya. You already know. Go on talking. Don't think of destinations. It is a long journey, as you remember."

"A long journey," I echoed.

But I did not want to talk. Bella had forced my thoughts back to the long, black years after Beatrice's death when the people's love of Lodovico had turned to hate and they had spat and cursed Lucrezia Crivelli when she rode through the streets at his side. Gian's murder was street gossip, Beatrice was spoken of in the hushed tones reserved for saints and popes and Lodovico was cast as the villain who overtaxed his people and betrayed his country to foreign armies.

Bella had pressed me to come with her to Naples after Atticus was buried and the French had taken over the city, but I was too afraid of my memories.

All our friends had gone, Leonardo to Venice, Sanseverino to seduce princes instead of marshalling troops to defend the city. We had lived badly under French rule. They took what little money there was left in the city and they treated the people like animals.

We all had wanted Lodovico to come back, and when he had returned from the Tyrol dressed like a prince in crimson damask and diamonds, I had wept with everybody else and had followed the crowds through the streets as they carried him on their shoulders to the cathedral to be blessed and reinstated. The French had fled, but they had held on to their main barracks in the Castello.

"Where are you, Catya? You look so sad."

I turned, startled, and looked at Bella.

"I was remembering when Lodovico came back, wondering at how quickly the people's minds changed again."

"They did not take long to put him out of favour after that, did they?" She laughed scornfully. "Poor fool. He should never have returned."

"Did you never pity him, Bella?"

"Pity? I despised him. He was such a coward, sitting crying in his bedroom while others went round doing his work for him. At least Beatrice had courage."

"Think how much he suffered."

"No more than I did in those long, weary years at Pavia."

"Your friends remained loyal," I said.

Her face hardened. "It is the price of power to have no friends. He should have remembered that."

I knew from experience and six years of these conversations that it was useless to argue with her. Two things we could never discuss in our friendship, her undying hatred of Lodovico and Beatrice, my knowledge that her family had murdered mine. I forced myself to stay silent now and went back to my thoughts.

I had pitied Lodovico with all my heart after his return to Milan. Perhaps Bella was right and he should have stayed in the Tyrol, for he was no longer the glorious prince that the Milanese remembered and looked to find again. They had suffered poverty and hardship under the French and Lodovico could only tax them more. The Emperor had taken the Duke's jewels in return for harbouring him, but nobody in Milan believed that and they bolted their doors against his agents when they went begging through the streets for money for the Duke. Lodovico had promised them riches and security and they expected it. Nobody wants a king when he is poor.

Lodovico was bewildered and broken by their attitude. He could not understand it.

I stayed because I thought he needed me. He had no friends left. Courtiers are all of the same breed. Just as they had deserted us when we most needed them at Maggiare, so they forgot the Duke's generosity and left him to fend for himself.

I was a fool to stay. The Estes had turned against Lodovico. They knew the circumstances of Beatrice's death. I had not forgotten Duke Ercole's face at her funeral. The Duke classed me with them.

I received a summons one day to his rooms above the Piazza del Castello. He gave me a small, cold nod instead of his usual easy smile and greeting, and then he handed me a letter. I knew the writing well and my spirits sank. It was from Isabella Gonzaga, one of the most cruelly polite documents I have ever read. The Duke had begged the Marquis of Mantua to help him beat back the French from their stronghold at Novara. Isabella wrote that, after careful consideration, they had decided to support the French King, since Mantua was too small a duchy to risk involvement in lost causes. I did not dare to look at Lodovico, but his words came as a shock.

"What do you have to say?" he asked abruptly. "You are one of them, Caterina."

"You know that to be untrue, my lord," I said slowly. "They treated me kindly and brought me up as one of them, but that was all."

"You are one of them," he repeated and buried his face in his hands. "God, the treachery that surrounds me. I thought of Isabella as my own sister. You will turn against me, too."

"No," I said, but he shook his head.

"How can I believe what any of you say? Even Sanseverino is talking of joining the French. I tell you, I trust nobody."

He raised his head and looked at me. "Go away, Caterina, back to Naples or Ferrara. I am tired of duplicity."

"Loyalty did you no good, Catya," Bella said. "I remember when you were forced to come to me for refuge after the Duke had banished you."

She shivered although the sun was hot on our faces. "Why did we start to talk of those years? They are better forgotten. I don't know why we live in courts, where all is treachery."

"We were born to them," I said. "We chose to stay in them and play their games. Just as you choose today to . . ."

"Do you want to go back?" said Bella, pulling up her horse across the path. "If you are afraid . . ."

"I am no coward," I said, "but I am frightened."

She dismounted and knotted the reins to a low-branched

tree overhanging the path. I followed suit. Hot and with the weight of age pulling like lead, we walked on slowly up the last hill, our shadows running ahead, crossing and lacing on the ground.

"It was important to do this," she said slowly. "I knew that you would not come here alone. I am certain that when you have conquered the past, you will find it easier to accept the future."

"Have you conquered yours?"

She kicked a stone out of the way. "No. I am afraid I have a less forgiving nature than you. There are two things in my life to which I shall never reconcile myself. I do not even want to, because it would seem like a betrayal. Gian's murder and the loss of my son."

"Have you heard any news of him?" I asked gently. I knew she did not like to talk of it.

She laughed bitterly. "The French King has put him into Holy Orders, safely out of the way."

"Why?"

"It means that he will never have a son who might have a better right to Milan than the King himself. Do you remember that day, Catya, after Lodovico had been captured, when we took my son to the Castello to see the King? What a fool I was!"

"How could you have known that the King would take him back to France? It was not your fault, Bella. We should not have trusted the French."

She nodded, but her face was full of grief.

"At least he is free," I said quickly. "Poor Lodovico has been imprisoned again, at Loches, I think."

"I wish you would stop indulging your pity for the man," she said angrily. "You talk of Lodovico and Beatrice as though they were saints. They were murderers, remember."

"Like your grandfather, Ferrante. Is that what you mean?"

"No! He was a good man, an honourable man. You shall not speak of him in the same breath."

"Oh, I agree with you," I said. "Will you never change, Bella? I am tired of your judgments on the people who were my friends. Your jealousy blinds you now, as it did then. Gian could never have ruled as they did. Never. Do you remember how the people wept when Beatrice died? How many tears were shed for Gian?"

"No, Catya." Bella put up her hand as if to ward off a blow. "I am sorry if I hurt you."

"I am used to it," I said. "You think that I have no feelings, that you can heap insults on Beatrice day after day, and yet you expect to be my friend."

"I have no others."

I hesitated, put a hand on her arm. "Bella, you have asked me to forget the past this afternoon."

"And you want me to do the same." She let her hand relax, brushed it across her face with a sigh. "What do we have to live on but our past? There is no future."

"Our daughters."

"What use are daughters? They can never be rulers."

"They can marry them."

She smiled at last. "True. Well, whom shall we choose? The King of Spain's son and François, the Dauphin?"

"Foreigners?"

She laughed at my shocked face. "What a patriot you are! Italy's day is over. You and I have seen it dying. Savonarola instead of the Medicis, Spanish popes and princes, French Lombardy."

I smiled at my own solemnity. "So long as Beatrice doesn't marry a Borgia, I shall be happy. That family horrifies me."

"But Lucrezia is almost your sister now," Bella said with a

malicious smile. "She has married Beatrice's brother, after all."

"I want nothing to do with them," I said firmly. "I hear that Isabella is making up to them, but then she is as amoral as they are."

"But are they so wicked as we are told?" Bella's voice was quick with interest. She loved scandalous gossip, for all her talk of propriety.

I tempted her. "Have you never heard of the Borgia Pope's banquet in Rome?"

"Tell me. Is it very horrible?"

"Oh, very," I said, laughing. "I am told that the Pope commanded a company of naked street women to join them, but they were kept on the floor, like dogs, while Lucrezia and Cesare sat with their father, throwing morsels of food down and making the poor ladies sit back on their haunches and bark their thanks before catching the crumbs in their mouths."

Bella nodded. "Now I know why the Pope died so horribly." She lowered her voice, although there was nobody to hear. "They say that his body swelled to three times its natural size and seven devils were clearly seen to come from him."

I burst out laughing. "How can you believe such rubbish . . ."

My voice trailed away into silence and I stood motionless on the path. She looked at me anxiously and took my arm.

"Only a few steps to the top of the hill," she said softly. "Be brave, Catya."

I twisted my fingers in my skirt. "I can't do it," I said. "Please don't make me."

My mother's body, lying in the sunny courtyard of Maggiare, broken like a cross. Red rivers running down between the cobbles. The cage over the gate, creaking and swinging with the weight of its load, the soldiers watching from the cloisters to see what the child would do.

"Quiet, Catya."

I opened my eyes as she looked down at me. "You screamed," she said. "Like a frightened child. I was wrong to bring you here. We will go back."

"No." I stood up, brushed the dust from my dress and managed to smile at her. "I would like to see Maggiare again."

"But there is nothing to see," she called after me as I walked on alone up the hill.

The valley was all sun and shadow, sun on the silver leaves of the olive trees, shadow on the dry river bed, turning the bleached stones to charcoal. Slowly I raised my eyes to the empty hillside. Three fat cows were chewing steadily at the short grass. So quiet, there was no other sound. A barren hill, one among many. Only the two orange trees that had once grown outside my bedroom window at Maggiare, shedding their white stars on the grass.

A shadow fell beside mine down the hill.

"Nothing left at all," I said slowly. "Not even a stone."

"Do you still regret having come here?" she asked looking at me.

I shook my head. "It is as if it had never been."

We watched the sun fade, the valley grow cold and black, and then we turned back towards Naples, our arms round each other to take us down the steep hill.